ECHOES OF WAR

Other books by this author available from New English Library:

Echoes of War

GEORGE G. GILMAN

NEW ENGLISH LIBRARY
TIMES MIRROR

for:
T. d'C.
Directly involved in my
favourite pursuits

A New English Library Original Publication 1977
© by George G. Gilman 1977

*

FIRST NEL PAPERBACK EDITION JULY 1977

*

NEL Books are published by
New English Library Limited from Barnard's Inn, Holborn, London EC1N 2JR
Made and printed in Great Britain by Hunt Barnard Printing Ltd., Aylesbury, Bucks.

45003175 6

CHAPTER ONE

A norther was blowing hard across the Iowa plains and over the Missouri. The sky was ugly to look at – grey with heavy black streaks. From time to time, showers of snow fell from the turbulent clouds and the wind seemed to howl with bitter glee at each shower, taking hold on the flakes and hurling them at anything solid which stood across its south-bound route.

Omaha was the major obstacle, crouching resolutely at the meeting point of the Platte with the Missouri: the first man-made hinderance of any size which the north-borne wind came across. To the east and south of the city the rivers raced and swirled, the brown surface of the waters scarred with angry white spume. On the streets and in the alleys, the white of drifted snow showed on the lee side of buildings. The instant it found shelter from the insistent tug of the wind, the snow became crusted with ice. Where there was no shelter, it slanted to the open ground only to be picked up again and hurled forward with even more force.

Between flurries, people with pressing business which forced them to be out on the streets cursed the cruel wind, its biting coldness and the acrid taint of smoke from the stacks of buildings and Union Pacific locomotives. Then, when the snow showers were unleashed, they cursed with more venom as the flakes became liquid on their clothing and soaked through to chill their flesh.

Some vented their feelings about the discomfort of the weather aloud. Some merely muttered. Others reflected their thoughts in expressions ranging from sullenness to anger.

One man smiled into the howling wind, unconcerned by the alternate discomforts of icy wetness and the swirling down-draught of the smoke. It was a quiet, easy-going smile: a match for his gait as he strolled east along the broad sidewalk of Douglas Street.

He was a tall man and the hunched shoulders and stooped

heads of everyone else hurrying back and forth on the north side of the street emphasised his height. For, without any sign of strain or rigidity, he carried his head high upon squared shoulders against the constant buffeting of the wind. In fact, he stood three inches over six feet and the casual way in which he made progress through the embryo blizzard was an indication of the easy strength commanded by his two-hundred-pound frame. It was a lean frame, not burdened with even an ounce of excess fat: but that was difficult to see as he covered the five block distance between the Astoria Hotel and the office of the Mid-West Steam Packet Company. For, from neck to knee, he was encased in a thick, fur-lined coat with the collar turned up to brush the underside of his low-crowned hat and buttoned from throat to mid-thigh.

But the face beneath the wide brim and between the standing collar gave a clue to the well-proportioned build that was concealed by the bulky coat. It was a lean face, the features angular – arranged in such a way that the man could be considered either handsome or ugly. Dominating the face was a pair of hooded eyes of crystal-clear blue. The cheek-bones were high and the jawline was firm; the skin stretched taut between. His nose had a hawklike quality, the nostrils slightly flared. Even though he was now smiling, his thin lips curled back to display well-shaped, very white teeth, and anyone who examined him closely would judge his mouthline to have a look of cruelty about it.

The frame of his face was comprised of thick, jet black hair which he wore long enough to brush his shoulders. The complexion was stained to a dark hue, the skin deeply scored by a network of lines: some etched by the passage of years to his present age, somewhere in the thirties but more cut by the harsh and bitter experiences he had endured over so many of those years.

While the set and colour of his face owed a great deal to the adult life he had led, his heritage had contributed more: for he was the result of a union between a Mexican father and a Scandinavian mother. The moustache which he wore, thick along his top lip and drooping to a point at each side of his mouth, emphasised the Latin blood-line. The crystal-clear blueness of his eyes made it obvious there was another strain running through his veins.

His name was Edge.

A new flurry of snow was hurled along Douglas Street as he

approached the corner of Fourteenth Street. His eyes, never wide, narrowed still more against the coldness of the rushing flakes. Visibility had been reduced to only a few feet, but Edge knew the office of the steamship company was on the corner of the intersection immediately ahead: and that he was passing a bakery store with a doorway set between two display windows.

As he drew level with the door, it was wrenched open and a middle-aged woman hurried out, a basket hooked over one arm as she struggled to open an umbrella. Edge caught a brief glimpse of her face beneath the brim of an oilskin hat: a gaunt, sour face made almost grotesquely ugly by a sprinkling of black warts and a moustache as thick as his own. Then the umbrella sprang open. The wind was gusting from behind her and she snarled an obscenity as the rush of air snapped the slats and ripped the fabric: but not before she had been lunged forward to slam into the solid bulk of Edge.

The half-breed withdrew both hands from his coat pockets, kept the woman from falling with one and touched the brim of his hat with the other.

'Long time since a woman threw herself at me, ma'am,' he said evenly, injecting humour into the contentment which formed his mouthline into a grin.

Anger emphasised the woman's homeliness as she wrenched herself out of Edge's firm grasp. 'Why don't you watch where you're goin'?' she snapped, fumbling with the ruined umbrella. 'What are you, drunk or somethin'? And it not yet ten o'clock in the mornin'!'

The narrow slits of Edge's blue eyes had never contributed anything to the smile: until now, as the woman hurled away the wrecked umbrella and glared her rage at all that ailed her towards him. The thin lips of the half-breed remained curled back, but altered their set slightly: and there was a brand of ice-like glitter in the eyes that set the seal on the cruelty latent behind the expression.

Fear emerged through the woman's anger and she took a backward step as the snow shower ended as abruptly as it had begun.

'That was two months ago in Frisco, ma'am,' Edge said. 'Guess you were just as ugly then. Today I'm sober.'

He touched the brim of his hat again and side-stepped to go around the shocked woman.

'Well, I never did!' she gasped, raising both hands to clutch at her scrawny throat.

'Nor never will, I figure,' Edge muttered with a final glance at the warts and unfeminine moustache. 'Something you got to face.'

The woman snorted her disgust and now seemed to welcome the wind as it helped to speed her retreat down the street. Edge, his features re-forming into the expression they had worn before the encounter with the woman, reached the doorway of the steamship company office. As he pushed open the solid wooden door, a four-seater roofed surrey turned in off Fourteenth Street and stopped at the kerb. He eyed the two passengers and driver with brief interest: in the way that he constantly maintained a surveillance on his surroundings. But the trio posed no overt threat and he stepped across the threshold and closed the door behind him.

The exposed flesh of his face immediately responded to the warmth of the stove in the office: losing the feeling of stiffness created by the biting coldness of the weather. A dozen people looked at him as he made his entrance: resentful that he had allowed a stream of icy air to sweep into the room. But it was immediately acknowledged that the discomfort was unavoidable and ten pairs of eyes ignored the newcomer. But a man and a woman merely pretended to lose interest in him: in fact, continued to cast surreptitious glances towards him as he unfastened the buttons of the coat and slackened the lanyard of his hat.

Aware of the covert attention he was receiving, the half-breed looked around him with the same degree of casual alertness that he had displayed since leaving the hotel a few minutes earlier. The room was about twenty feet square, the rear third of its area partitioned off by a counter. There was a desk, a chair and a safe behind the counter. The shirt-sleeved clerk seemed disgruntled that he was not sitting at the desk: and his youthful, red blotched face expressed more displeasure than anyone else's on Edge's arrival. For it meant that he had to stand behind the counter that much longer, issuing tickets and receiving payment.

The would-be passengers stood in an orderly line, along the counter and around the angle of a side wall. Their enjoyment of the warmth emanating from the pot-bellied stove in the centre of the public area of the room was marred by the steam rising from their wet topclothes.

Pools of water lay on the bare wooden boards of the floor. The paint on the walls was peeling and the counter was scratched and burned. Dull looking timetables of the services between St Louis and Fort Bulford and over-coloured paintings of scenes along the route were hung on the walls. On the counter, to either side of the clerk, were piles of papers. At one end was a model of a stern-wheeler protected by a smeared glass dome.

The room smelled of dampness, old cigar smoke and fresh coffee. The clerk interrupted the issue of a ticket to delve under the counter and bring up a mug, which he drank from. It didn't improve his mood.

Under the fur-lined coat, Edge wore black pants, a grey shirt, black kerchief and a gunbelt. In the holster tied down to his right thigh there was a slimbutted .44–40 Remington revolver: as brand new as his clothing. But, after failing to see any sign of potential danger, he allowed his coat to swing back and cover the gun.

Of those in the line ahead of him, two were women and the rest men. All of them were middle-aged to elderly with the exception of the woman who had been unable to conceal her curiosity about him. She was in her mid-twenties, an attractive brunette wearing a long coat belted tightly at the waist which hinted at a fine figure. The man immediately behind her in the line was the other party who had shown more than a passing interest in Edge. He was short and fleshy, with a freckled face and hair that was both greying and thinning. In his late forties, he was nervous and had taken off his derby hat so that his constantly moving hands could toy with it.

His interest in the half-breed had been fearful, and remained so until he forced his attention away to concentrate on nothing. The woman had been startled, but only for a moment. Then she calmed and although she continued to shoot fast glances back along the line, the expression in her green eyes held an odd mixture of coyness and frank appraisal – until her gaze was fleetingly trapped by the glittering coldness in the half-breed's eyes. Then she flushed crimson from the roots of her hair to the point where her slender neck plunged from sight behind the collar of her coat.

Only a few seconds had elapsed and the room temperature had not yet climbed back up to where it had been before Edge entered. But he was beginning to relish the warmth and was amongst those who shivered when the door opened to

9

admit a new stream of snow-chilled air. Every eye shifted towards the trio of newcomers: resentfully, fearfully and carefully.

But there was nothing about the entrance of the three men to arouse suspicion. They came in backwards, taking off their hats and shaking them as if to rid them of snowflakes out on the sidewalk rather than inside. From their long black coats with collars turned high about their ears, Edge recognised them as the men from the surrey.

'Shut out that damn weather!' the clerk yelled irritably.

Edge had started to lose interest in the newcomers as they backed into the office, banging into each other in their apparent haste to get out of the wind and snow.

'Sonny, how would you like another hole in your head?'

The threat was yelled, the opening words competing with the sound of the howling wind. Then the door was kicked shut and the voice was heard to have a muffled quality.

The trio whirled, the man at either side moving to give room to the one in the middle. Each face was masked by a kerchief from just below the eyes. As if they were performing a well-rehearsed trick, the men replaced the Stetsons on their heads with their left hands while their right arms whipped down from under the hats and thrust forward. The man in the centre, who had snarled the retort at the clerk, was clutching a combination pistol, knife and knuckleduster with the blade extended and a finger curled around the trigger. The man on his right had an over-and-under Derringer: the one on his left an English .43 Trantor double-action five-shot.

'Oh, no!' the balding, greying fat man gasped, nearly collapsing into a faint of fear but managing to find the support of the wall.

The clerk, who had been about to sip more coffee, vented a squeal like a hurt cat and dropped his mug. It hit the counter top spraying the papers with liquid.

Only for part of a second did Edge consider going for his gun. But he got no further than curling the long, brown-skinned fingers of his right hand under the flap of his coat.

'I wouldn't, mister!' the man with the Trantor snapped, raking the gun around to cover the half-breed.

The eyes of the other two men covered the rest of the line and the clerk between them: and saw that fear swamped any inclination towards retaliation.

'Gives us something in common, feller,' Edge answered. 'I wouldn't either.'

He started to drop his hand to his side. But then he raised it: slowly, to find the lobe of his right ear and tug at it.

'Wise man.'

The one with the Derringer moved forward, taking long strides towards the counter. The clerk seemed transfixed to the floor. Tears squeezed from his eyes and ran slowly over the curves of his blotchy cheeks as the small gun drew a bead on the centre of his forehead.

'Every cent you have,' the gunman said, his tone pleasant, perhaps even a little girlish. He drew a burlap sack from his coat pocket and dropped it on the counter. 'In here.'

The clerk flapped his mouth open and shut but made no sound. Until the double muzzle of the tiny gun was pushed forward to rest on the sweat-sheened skin of his brow. 'Hole'll be here,' the gunman encouraged. 'If you have any troubles, they'll be over.'

The youngster squealed again, snatched up the sack and whirled to stagger towards the safe.

'You folks have your valuables ready,' the man with the three-in-one weapon announced calmly. 'Sack will be passed along. Just like in church, Sunday. Give generously, or give your all. You appreciate what I am saying to you?'

'Yes. Yes, most certainly!' the short, fat man spluttered. Now that the hold-up was underway, he had overcome his nerves and recovered from the near faint. He looked and sounded relieved as he fumbled to unfasten his coat.

'Appreciate your attitude!' the man with his back to the door said quickly, his tone harsh as he swung the odd weapon towards the co-operative man. 'But slow and easy. My friends and I are a trifle nervous. Be a shame to kill somebody for no reason.'

Fear was like a palpable presence in the room, augmenting the heat from the stove to draw sweat from almost every pore: captors and captives alike. Body odour became the most pungent smell.

'Something you should know, feller,' Edge said to the man who covered him with the Trantor.

'Always willing to learn.'

'We ever meet up again, don't point a gun at me – unless you figure to kill me. I don't like guns aimed at me. Always give folks one warning about that.'

11

'Tall, broad and hard nosed,' the man responded lightly. 'I hope your bankroll is as big as your courage, mister.'

Edge shook his head. 'The money's not important. Warning is.'

'Speak for yourself, mister,' the man snapped, and inched the gun further ahead of him. 'Give out the roll. Slow, with your hand wide of the gun.'

The clerk had transferred money from the safe to the sack. Back at the counter, he took more cash from a drawer beneath and added this. When he tried to hand the sack back to the gunman, it was waved away, towards the first would-be passenger in the line. Then the little under-and-over followed the sack from person to person, halting when it did. Bills, coins and jewellery were dropped into the mouth of the sack.

'Been nice up to now,' the man with the Derringer said pleasantly. 'Keep it going like that and there won't be any blood on anyone's hands.'

The man with his back to the door was becoming increasingly nervous. His kerchief was black, but it showed the stains of sweat soaking through from his cheeks. His dark eyes moved constantly in their sockets, as his strange weapon raked back and forth along the line.

'Save your mouth for what it's best at, Jase!' he snapped.

'Very nice!' the man with the Derringer responded, speaking the words in a tone of pouting injury.

Edge had eased a folded stack of bills from his hip pocket and swung his arm wide so that his hand stayed clear of the Remington butt. He transferred the money to his left hand and resumed tugging at his ear lobe with the right. When the sack was extended towards him by the man next in line, he dropped the bankroll into it.

The masked man with the Derringer was still smarting under the taunt directed at him. His stride was as angry as his gaze as he approached the end of the line on a curving course, holding out his free hand to take the sack. The way he walked and the motion of his hips was as girlish as his tone had been earlier. The sack was pushed out towards him and he snatched at it angrily.

Edge moved his hand away from his ear and into the long hair at the nape of his neck, as if to scratch at the source of an itch.

Then, in a blur of speed, the hand streaked away from his shoulder.

'Jase!' the man backed to the door shrieked. 'Don't, Scott!'

Edge didn't move his feet, because the petulent Jase made it unnecessary. He took the sack blind, his hurt and angry gaze fixed upon the man at the door. Thus, he was unaware of danger until it was too late. Both the man with the combination weapon and the one named Scott stared in horror at Edge, and this warned Jase where the threat lay. But, even as he whipped his head around to look at Edge – raking his tiny gun in the same direction – the half-breed fastened a grip on him.

It was Edge's left hand that clawed on to Jase's left shoulder. His right wrist was already extended at the full stretch of his arm: to rest the blade of a straight razor against the man's right temple – a fraction of an inch away from his eye. Then, even before the man at the door yelled the order – sounding more like a plea – to Scott, Edge jerked Jase towards him.

Jase was unbalanced and could not resist. He moved fast to the side, slamming to a halt against the towering leanness of Edge. The razor tracked him, pressed hard enough against the target of flesh to nick the skin without drawing blood.

It had all happened in less than a second and for half that time the half-breed had been exposed to a killing shot blasted from the Trantor of Scott. But Scott wasted his chance by thinking about it and, by the time he had decided to ignore his order, Jase was between the Trantor and Edge: and under threat of having his eye gouged out by a blade which had seemed to appear from thin air.

'Oh, my sweet Jesus!' a man rasped softly.

The Trantor continued to be aimed at the suddenly trembling Jase. The combination weapon had wavered during the flurry of activity, but now began to track up and down the line of still exposed hostages. Both these hold-up men had recovered from the shock and their eyes above the masks were hard with grim determination. Jase was weak with terror and he dropped both the sack and the Derringer, the burlap and metal slipping from shaking, sweat-greased hands.

'I'll kill one for every second you don't let Jase go!' the man with his back to the door growled thickly, his voice having to rasp over the flesh of a dry throat and mouth before forcing a way through the mask.

Scott raised the Trantor to sight along the length of his rock-steady arm. His aim was at Edge's impassive face above Jase's left shoulder.

'Surrender, please!' the elderly woman in the line begged.

There was fear behind the unflinching face of the tall half-breed: far behind, buried deep in the pit of his stomach. He had faced death a thousand times in as many different situations and, long ago, he had been prepared to meet his maker without enduring the torment of such fear. But his youth had passed and with it had gone a naïve belief in fate. A cruel fate that had appeared to map out a destiny for him – ensuring that he survived every danger so that he should live to suffer the brutal consequences.

'They're a couple of fruits, ma'am,' Edge said evenly. 'And this one's ripe to be cut open.'

For a long time now he had regarded fear as a weapon: as essential to survival as his skill with gun and blade. For, if it was controlled, fear was a guard against recklessness and also acted to sharpen a man's wits and reflexes. As he stood now, in the overheated office, it was the cold fear in the pit of his stomach that made the largest contribution to his icy calm.

'Henry, he's got me cold!' Jase pleaded.

'And a sneeze could be fatal,' Edge warned.

Henry had halted the raking action of his strange gun to aim it steadily at the woman who had called on Edge to surrender. The knuckle of his trigger finger was white with the strain of holding first pressure.

'I'm no fruit!' Scott snarled, his revolver wavering slightly in its aim at the half-breed's head.

'But I figure you're in the same jam as the others, feller,' Edge replied evenly.

Henry reached his decision and pushed his free hand behind him to grasp the doorknob. 'All right, we're leaving! But you better see Jase gets arrested in one piece, mister! Beat it, Scott!'

He turned the knob and stepped forward: to avoid being slammed in the back as the wind folded the door inwards. His gun swept around to aim towards Jase and Edge.

'Frigging freak amateurs!' Scott snarled, anger and hatred doing battle for command of the exposed part of his face.

But he whirled and lunged for the open doorway as the wind howled and gusted, to billow a shower of snow into the office.

'Only my money I want to keep,' Edge muttered, and raised his knee as he shoved Jase forward with the hand on the man's shoulder.

14

Jase yelled in alarm as he felt himself moving. Then the sound became a scream of pain as the knee was slammed into the small of his back to drive him faster towards the door.

Scott whipped his head around, his Trantor lagging behind. Henry swung his gun.

'I'm all right!' Jase shrieked, screwing his head around to make sure.

He saw the razor in mid-air, tossed by Edge's right hand to his waiting left. The half-breed's right was already fisted around the butt of the Remington and had the gun clear of the holster, his thumb cocking the hammer.

'Two points loses,' Edge growled as the Trantor's muzzle drew a bead on him. He squeezed the trigger of the Remington.

Scott did not have time to alter his expression. He was enraged at himself, his two companions and Edge for the way the hold-up had gone wrong. The fire in his blazing eyes seemed capable of melting the snow that rushed in through the doorway to whiten everything in its path. And he died in the grip of the anger, as the bullet from Edge's rock-steady gun exploded into his heart.

He took one step backwards, then fell. The Trantor slipped from his spasming hand. His eyes remained wide above the mask, and became misted with the dull glaze of death. He sprawled backwards across the storm-ravaged threshold of the office. The blossoming stain on the front of his coat froze and then, like the rest of his body, was spread with a concealing mantle of pure white. Then immediately this was sprinkled with a fine rain of bright crimson as a second gunshot blasted across the office.

Jase, thrust across the floor by the half-breed's knee, banged into Henry. Both men cursed – Henry's oath the shriller and more obscene as his attempt to use the revolver action of his weapon was spoiled by the collision. Then Jase died, as an area of his back from shoulder-blades to the base of his spine became an awesome crater: its sides a bright, fluid crimson against which chips of shattered bone showed as gleams of white.

The force of the blast threw the corpse against Henry and drove the living man out on to the sidewalk at a backward run. Jase collapsed then, his lifeless body crumpling to sprawl beside the inert form of Scott. Wind-driven snow had already masked the sprinkling of blood which had splashed the first man to die. Now it began to fill the great hole in the back of the second corpse.

As the bitterly cold air rushing in through the doorway cleaned the stink of burnt powder from the office, Edge started forward and glanced to his right. He saw the clerk's head appear above the counter top, the red blotches on his face more pronounced now that the rest of his skin was deathly pale with naked fear. Below his head, there was a jagged hole in the front of the counter, where the shotgun had been blasted out of cover.

Excited talk erupted and a woman screamed. Edge reached the doorway and stepped across both snow-covered bodies to rake his narrow-eyed gaze along the street. The shower ended and the flakes which had fallen were driven low across the broad intersection of Douglas and Fourteenth. Henry was halfway across the crossroads, running fast. He slipped and fell hard. His hat came free of his head and was claimed by the wind. As the fleeing man sprang to his feet, Edge caught a brief glimpse of his face. The mask had been wrenched down, but the half-breed captured only a momentary impression of pale skin and dark, red-rimmed eyes. Then the man was up and running again, but with less haste. His left leg was dragged and favoured.

The horse in the shafts of the surrey eyed Edge balefully. Slack traffic moved slowly up and down Douglas. A few hurrying pedestrians showed no interest in the doorway of the steamship company office.

'He's gone?' the clerk asked, and gulped, as the half-breed turned to step back over the bodies.

Edge pushed the Remington back into the holster as his boots crunched on frozen snow. Then eased the razor out of sight under the long hair at the nape of his neck. It went, still open, into a leather pouch that extended several inches down the line of his spine: the pouch held in place by a beaded thong encircling his neck under a kerchief.

'Be in Nebraska City by noon if he don't slow down,' the half-breed replied as he stooped to pick up the burlap sack. He took his bankroll out and dropped the sack to the floor again. Then moved to take his former position at the end of the line.

For a few moments the clerk and ten of the would-be passengers continued to express varying degrees of shock and fear. The pretty brunette and the short fat man looked at

16

Edge with unconcealed admiration.

Then a man broke from the line to go for the sack. The others who had property to reclaim did likewise. Edge moved forward to the counter.

'One way to Bismarck on the first available boat, feller,' the half-breed asked, his bankroll still in his hand.

The clerk had moved to peer around the tall, lean figure: his blotchy face anxious as he watched people delve into the sack. His eyes were cracked against the wind which continued to rush into the office, through a door which could not be closed because of the rapidly stiffening bodies across the threshold.

'The hell with that, mister!' the youngster snapped. 'I got company money to get back. And a crime to report.'

He started to move away, towards a section of the counter which could be raised and opened. But he halted abruptly, as Edge thrust out an arm and fastened a strong grip on his shoulder. Fearful some of the people might take more than they were entitled to from the sack, the clerk shot an angry glance at Edge and made to jerk free of the hand hold. But then he did a double take at the lean, dark-skinned face. And fear filled his eyes again: for the half-breed's features were set in an expression of ice-cold anger – the eyes mere slits of glinting blue and the lips curled just fractionally to display the serrated line where his upper and lower teeth met. The grip on his shoulder tightened to a point where the clerk grimaced with pain.

'One way to Bismarck, feller. On the first boat to leave.' Edge's lips hardly moved to repeat his request.

'All right,' the clerk rasped through his clenched teeth. 'But what's the damn hurry? *Delta Dawn* don't leave until two this afternoon. Maybe not even then if the blizzard's still blowin'.'

Edge nodded and withdrew his hand, 'Obliged.'

'No private compartments left,' the clerk growled as he massaged his pained shoulder. 'You'll have to bunk in with the roustabouts or wait for the next boat.'

'I ain't proud, feller.'

'Just in an all-fire hurry!' The clerk avoided looking at Edge and concentrated on issuing the ticket.

'Cold is all,' the half-breed replied evenly, his face resuming its impassive set.

'Right through to your heart, sir!' an elderly man in stovepipe hat and Ulster coat pronounced emphatically, as he thudded the sack on to the counter. It was still bulky with steamship company money. 'I am certain those three misguided souls would have retreated under the mere threat of your gun. There was no need for violence.' He spun on his heels and held his hat on his head as he went towards the door. 'And I intend to tell the authorities of my contention.'

He ducked his head into the gusting wind as he stepped gingerly over the bodies. The clerk handed Edge his ticket and accepted payment, then eagerly grabbed the sack. The half-breed refastened his coat as he turned and started for the door.

'There are some of us who are grateful to you for what you did,' the elder of the two women offered. 'My husband and I could ill-afford to lose what they attempted to take from us.'

'Nonsense, Hannah!' the sour-faced man with her exclaimed. 'We could all have been killed! He cared only about himself and his loss!'

'That is beside the point!' the younger woman argued, with some vehemence in her tone. 'It was only the criminals who suffered and none of us lost anything.'

Edge was about to step across the bodies when his way was blocked by the man in a stove-pipe hat and a beefy deputy town marshal. The lawman was wearing a bulky top-coat, but had a gunbelt slung around his hips on top. His badge of a star in a circle was pinned to his left lapel. He dropped a hand to drape the butt of a holstered Colt when he saw Edge.

'That's him, officer!'

The deputy ignored the man at his side. He stood as solidly as a marble statue in the forceful wind. His hard, unblinking eyes had taken in the scene at a single glance. 'Where the hell you goin'?'

'Bismarck,' Edge answered and vented a low sigh. 'Later, I guess?'

The lawman gave a curt nod and shifted a slower gaze around the people behind the half-breed. 'Ain't no one goes anyplace until the law's business is done.' He blinked now, as he refixed his gaze on Edge and waved a hand towards the two bodies. 'You put these two guys in cold-store?'

The half-breed stepped to the side, out of the full force of the wind gusting through the doorway. 'If you want to talk shop, feller – one bought it from my draw: the other got it from under the counter.'

18

CHAPTER TWO

The norther blew itself into extinction shortly before noon and a bright sun broke through the abruptly slow-moving clouds and pushed them into a bank over in the east. But with the brightness came a new low degree of cold. The still air had a static forcefulness of its own that pressed through the warmest clothing to chill the flesh and seemed to reach beneath and touch a man's bones.

Standing on the Hurricane Deck of the stern-wheeler *Delta Dawn*, moored at a downtown Omaha wharf, Edge was able to ignore the intense cold. By the simple expedient of accepting it as one more passing facet of harshness in a life destined to be filled with suffering.

On all sides, there was noise and bustle. Aboard the steamship, roustabouts kept the cold at bay by stacking cargo in the forward hold. The capstan engine at the bow whined and the derrick swung back and forth. On the wharf, stevedores worked up a sweat of their own handling the freight designated to go aboard the *Delta Dawn*. Moored fore and aft of the stern-wheeler were other steamers preparing to leave, attended by the same hectic activity.

Beyond the wharf, Omaha was bustling again after the morning blizzard: busy with the business of making money from being a centre of both rail and river traffic.

The Missouri was calm and stained dark brown with mud again, flowing with slow majesty under the arches of the railroad bridge – except where side- and stern-wheelers, keelboats, yawls and mackinaws trailed white wakes or thrashed the surface into a bubbling turmoil.

The tall, lean man with his hands thrust deep into the pockets of the fur-lined coat did not ignore his surroundings. But anyone who studied him for any length of time might have thought it was sheer boredom which caused him to glance lazily around from time to time: breaking off from his impassive contemplation of the rolling Iowa countryside beyond Council Bluffs on the far side of the river.

Both the best times and perhaps the very worst of his life had been over there: further than he could see from the boat – in the state's corn belt where the Hedges' farm had been. The good times before the War Between the States, when his parents were alive and even after they were dead, continuing to work the place with his kid brother, Jamie.

His part in the war had been staged much further east: fighting for a cause and then for sheer survival on the battlefields of Virginia, Tennessee, the Carolinas and Georgia. He went to war as a naïve farm boy and became through his experience as a soldier, a hard and embittered man. But, as he rode westwards from Appomattox towards the farm and Jamie he knew he was capable of leaving the past and its harshest experiences behind him.

Until he found the farm a burnt-out shell, its fields charred black and the mutilated body of his brother providing a meal for buzzards.

At that time in his life, the man who was now called Edge had not learned how to cool burning anger. One of Jamie's killers was also feeding the buzzards that day: and provided the clue that led south towards the Mexican border – where the man returned from the war expunged his uncontrolled anger by using the unforgotten lessons of war to take his revenge against the murderers of his brother. Five men who, like the one who died alongside Jamie, had served in the Union cavalry troop commanded by Captain Josiah C. Hedges.

Kansas had been crossed on the route of his vengeance ride south and a man had died there: because he misjudged the mood and skills of the tall, lean, revenge-hungry half-breed. And, when the wanted posters were issued, a Mexican mispronounced the name Hedges to provide a killer with a new one.

Many other men had died violently at the hand of Edge since the life-blood of Elliot Thombs was spilled on the rich soil of Kansas. Between that far-off day and this morning, when his newly purchased gun blasted the life from the hold-up man, perhaps he had killed more men than he had slaughtered for the cause and for his survival during the war.

But there were no wanted posters out on the man called Edge. Many men and some women had blamed him on the grounds of morality – much as the old-timer in the stove-pipe

20

hat had berated him this morning. However, the law had always been forced to hold its hand, if not its representatives' tongues. Just as the beefy deputy town marshal had been required to do earlier, after listening to eye-witness accounts of the hold-up and its blood-spattered finale.

There had been shattered bodies and spurting crimson on the final leg of Edge's aimless journey which had so far led him from the burnt-out Iowa farm to the winter coldness of Omaha. The men who had been killed because they had attempted to prevent the half-breed completing a job he had been hired to do. He did not complete the job in the manner expected of him: but he did finish it to his own satisfaction – and received the thousand-dollar pay-off he was promised in San Francisco.

It was that thousand dollars which financed his stay at the Astoria Hotel, purchased his new clothes and hand-gun and bought the ticket on the *Delta Dawn*, on the Hurricane Deck of which he stood now: reflecting on the past without regret, ignoring the future and betraying no indication of how closely he was examining his surroundings of the present.

For danger dogged him more closely than his shadow at high noon. Through almost every state and territory west of the Mississippi it had never been more than a gunshot away from whichever course he had chosen to wander – or somebody had paid him money to take. And the key to his survival – for it was essential if he were to have the opportunity to use his skill with blade or gun – was his war-taught ability to be on his guard against danger every second, even when asleep.

Thus, he was not startled when a hand tapped him lightly on the shoulder.

'The old lady's husband was right, ma'am,' he said evenly. 'I did it for me and my money.'

'It doesn't matter,' the pretty brunette who had been in the office of the Mid-West Steam Packet Company answered with a shrug. 'I've already had my say about that to the deputy marshal. I was just going to offer a penny for your thoughts.'

Since climbing the main stairway to the raised deck, Edge had been aware of the passage of time. A clock somewhere in midtown Omaha had marked each quarter hour with pleasant chimes which cut through the more raucous sounds of commerce and industry. From one-thirty, officers, crewmen and passengers had been boarding the stern-wheeler. And the clock was chiming a quarter past two when he saw the woman

21

moving up the gangplank from the wharf. She had caught his eye for a moment, then was apparently ignored. But he continued to be aware of her as she organised the carrying of two large trunks into a passenger compartment amidships: and sensed her approach from behind before she tapped him on the shoulder.

'Nothing I want costs only a penny,' he told her, and she flushed again, as his cold eyes surveyed her with complete frankness.

Out in the bright sunlight her features were as attractive to look at as they had been in the gloom of the office. Even more so, he thought: perhaps because she had taken off her hat so that her coal black hair – sheened and fine – fell freely to below her shoulders in a series of natural waves. When she tried to hide her embarrassment behind a smile, she showed two crooked teeth which detracted from her beauty but added character to her otherwise perfect face.

'My name is Charity Meagher and I'm going all the way to Fort Bulford on this boat. Then overland to a town called Lisaville on the Musselshell River. I'm hired to teach school there.'

She spoke slowly and distinctly, not enjoying the half-breed's impassive survey of her face and thickly cloaked body: but using the time to rid her skin of the blush.

'I like children, don't you, Mr Edge? I always have, ever since I discovered I wasn't a child anymore.'

Edge showed a quiet smile now – just a little warmer than the one he had worn before the ugly old lady had broken his mood of contentment that morning. 'Glad to see it was a discovery that's been well-developed, ma'am,' he responded softly, his gaze shifting from the conical mounds of her heavily shrouded breasts to her face.

Dull red suffused her from hairline to throat once again. 'Oh dear, you're flirting with me!' she said in a hushed whisper.

'Maybe, ma'am. But you happen to look better than Iowa to me right now. And a whole lot fresher.'

The smile had gone from his face and his tone was flat. His abrupt change of mood – back to what it had been before she approached him – both surprised and disturbed her. The expression on her own face became sympathetic.

'Bad memories, Mr Edge?'

He was looking out across the river again. 'My business.'

22

The curt response stirred her to the beginnings of anger. 'You brought it up!'

'Happens sometimes.' He put his back to the Missouri and all that lay on the other side and shifted his casually careful attention to the wharf. The *Delta Dawn* and the other moored boats were still being loaded with cargo, the tempo of the work increasing as departure time approached for all three. Passengers and people who had come to see them off thronged the wharf. 'You still want to talk, ma'am?'

'I love to,' Charity replied, encouraged.

Edge showed her another brief smile that was as close as he ever got to a broad grin. 'So let's do that.'

The colour rushed to her cheeks: but spread no further and was not so deep as before. 'You really are a very strange man, aren't you?' she posed rhetorically as Edge resumed his surveillance of the busy scene on the dockside.

He paid particular attention to a tall, slender, almost graceful man who was wandering through the crowd with apparent aimlessness. The man was well dressed in high-buttoned boots, a tailored topcoat, cravat and derby worn at a jaunty angle. His face was very pale, like that of a man who spent most of his time indoors. It was a long, rather mournful face with deepset blue eyes, hollow cheeks, aquiline nose and thin mouth above a weak jaw.

'Like everyone else, ma'am, I think I'm normal,' Edge replied at length, not sure if he was telling the truth or not. There was something familiar about the well-dressed man with the wan face. Not so much in his build, but rather the set of his almost characterless features.

'I sometimes think I'm not like other women,' Charity said. 'Especially in a situation such as this.'

'You can do all right if you try hard enough,' the half-breed told her. 'How did you play it with the clerk at the office?'

'I don't know what you mean.'

The pale-faced man lifted a billfold from the side pocket of a grey-haired old-timer: then moved away with calm innocence. And Edge saw why his gait was not as graceful as it should have been. He limped slightly, favouring his left leg.

'Clerk told me there were no cabins left. Way things happened, you didn't get service until after me. And you got a cabin.'

Edge saw the limping man lift a pocket-book from a basket

held by a middle-aged woman deep in fast conversation with another woman. Then the half-breed's attention was captured by a fellow-passenger who carried a bulky carpet-bag across the Hurricane Deck. It was the short, overweight, greying man who had been in the shipping company office during the hold-up. The man paid no heed to Edge or Charity Meagher as he made a beeline for the cabin next to that of the woman and went inside.

'*He* didn't use feminine charm, that's for sure,' Edge muttered sourly as the *Delta Dawn*'s steam whistle shrilled and preparations were made to haul up the gangplank and release the mooring lines.

'That is Mr Horace Ferris,' Charity supplied.

'Guess it's just because he's a big wheel, uh?'

'Excuse me?'

'Ferris – a big wheel?'

'A well-known businessman in New Orleans.' She was suddenly tight-lipped. 'And there was no favouritism on the part of the clerk, Mr Edge. I can assure you of that. Mr Ferris and I booked ahead for our cabins. We were merely in the office to confirm our bookings.' There was a note of triumph in her voice now. 'Your mistake, I think?'

'Nobody's perfect, ma'am.'

The half-breed was studying the pale-faced man again. He was certain it was Henry. Once the fact of the limp was established, the rest of the man's physical appearance provided a match. The only difference was that Henry had changed his topclothes. But this did not account for Edge's vague feeling of recognition of the man: a feeling he had first sensed from looking at Henry's face. In the office, the face had been effectively masked: then, out on the intersection, there had been just a distant glimpse which conveyed no detail. So, the half-breed decided, the total memory of the pale-faced Henry was locked deep in the back of his mind. Stored in that lobe of his brain that seldom revealed its secret hoard – unless something in the present reminded him strongly of the past.

Like a view of Iowa stirring up memories of Jamie; or boat wakes scarring the muddy Missouri recalling San Francisco Bay where the slaughter road to Omaha had begun: or even Charity Meagher triggering to the forefront of his mind another period of the past he hardly ever thought about.

'Have you ever been married, Mr Edge?' the woman asked suddenly, almost as if she had read the thought which flashed

24

through his mind: and therefore knew the answer to the question.

'Thief!' a man shrieked. 'I've been robbed! Stop that sonof-abitch!'

Edge saw Henry lift leather for a third time – delving under the lapel of a middle-aged man preoccupied in waving to somebody aboard the boat berthed ahead of the *Delta Dawn*. But, in withdrawing his hand, Henry's coat cuff caught on a watch chain and the movement alerted the victim.

The boats fore and aft had already cast off their mooring lines and their bows were swinging out towards mid-river, helms held hard over to steer on to a south-bound course. Their stern-wheels thrashed brown water to white foam, their engines thudded, their whistles shrilled in high-pitched warnings and their spare steam hissed through the safety-valves. Bells rang and orders were yelled. On boats and wharf, passengers and those who had come to see them off shouted last minute good-byes.

The half-breed had been about to snap his head around and snarl at the woman to mind her own business. But the abrupt burst of excitement amid bustle on the dockside saved Charity from the retort. For Edge kept his attention directed towards Henry, as the hold-up man turned pickpocket whirled from his victim and sprinted away.

For a moment, nobody else was aware of the crime and its discovery. Then, as Henry zig-zagged through the crowd, banging into people and knocking bags and packages to the ground, the meaning of the victim's words as well as the sound of his voice reached other ears.

'Me, too!' a woman shrieked. 'I've been robbed!'

The man who had raised the alarm gave chase, yelling for Henry to be stopped and held. A few men made half-hearted attempts to comply, and two beefy stevedores went for full-blooded tackles. But Henry was too agile for them and they found themselves grappling each other as they slammed to the ground with yells of anger and pain. Most people scuttled from the weaving path of the fleeing pick-pocket.

The *Delta Dawn* was no longer moored to the wharf. Both her fore and her aft lines had been cast off, but the helmsman and pilot were holding her tight to the dockside with the wheel hard over and the engines alternately in drive and reverse. For the boat ahead had not yet made her turn to steam down-river and was blocking the way. But, despite the efforts in the wheel-house and engine-room, the flow of the Missouri relentlessly inched the bow of the *Delta Dawn* away from the wharf. Then she was jutting out at a forty-five degree angle, her stern gunwale creaking against the dock pilings, when Henry realised the departing boat offered his only means of escape. For the stevedores had picked themselves up – one to give chase and the second to sprint for a blocking position. Their voices, raised to a harsh pitch to curse at Henry and anybody who stood in their way, attracted the attention of others of their kind.

'Ten dollars to the man who gets the bastard!' Henry's last victim snarled.

'I'll match that!' the woman who had been robbed added shrilly.

Whistles blasted, engines thudded and paddle-wheels thrashed. But the offers of reward were heard and passed on. The thief was heading diagonally across the wharf, aiming for an area of warehouses which promised cover to throw off his pursuers before he lost himself in the riverside section of town.

Abruptly, a half dozen dock workers emerged from one of the warehouses, saw the hue and cry, heard the money talk and spread out: cutting off Henry's escape route and brandishing bill-hooks.

Edge and everyone else aboard the *Delta Dawn* had only a rear view of Henry when the running man realised he was trapped. But then Henry leaned into a fast turn – to duck under the outstretched arms of the stevedore intent upon tackling him before he reached the workers waiting at the warehouses. People shuffled and leapt out of Henry's new path, enjoying the chase now: loyalties divided between the quarry and his pursuers. Henry's face, which could now be seen by those aboard the stern-wheeler, showed an expression of mild anxiety for a moment. But then became spread with a broad grin of satisfaction when he saw that the *Delta Dawn* had not yet lost contact with the wharf.

Charity gripped Edge's upper arm tightly and exclaimed: 'That man, isn't he the one . . . ?'

'Looks like it could be second time lucky,' Edge answered.

The boat ahead thrashed clear of the *Delta Dawn*'s course and the boarding of the Hurricane Deck trembled as the engines were throttled to full ahead.

The steam whistle shrilled and open water showed between

the entire length of the hull and the wharf.

Henry spurted and the stevedore who had been behind him now lunged out from a group of excited watchers ahead of him. Without breaking stride or hindering his balance, Henry delved a hand under the left lapel of his coat and withdrew it. A flash of sunlight showed across his clenched fist. The stevedore crouched and leaned forward, pushing out his arms to full stretch. Henry ran directly into the start of a body-crushing bearhug.

Witnesses howled for blood or snarled their displeasure that the chase was to end so quickly.

Henry held up his left arm in what seemed to be an in-effectual defence against the trap of the stevedore's arms. But his left swung in the arc of an uppercut. The brass knuckle-dusters of his combination weapon flashed once again in the cold sunlight: and the stevedore was suddenly flat on his back – his mouth sagged crookedly open in the sculpture of a broken jaw. Blood, sprinkled with the white flotsam of frag-ments of broken teeth, bubbled up and spilled over his lower lip.

Howls of enraged protest were mixed with cheers of ap-proval.

Again, Henry did not break stride. His leading foot slammed down on to the belly of the unconscious man and the yielding flesh acted as a springboard to power his final dash to the lip of the wharf. The crowds moved further back on either side. Henry angled slightly to the left – to head for the point where the gap between boat and dockside was narrowest.

He leapt clear, head high and feet pedalling in mid-air. Every passenger aboard the *Delta Dawn* – save one – surged forward to the rails of the various decks. And saw Henry slam to the safety of the wheel support. The leap was across more than seven feet of open water and Henry vented a shriek of pain as the impact punished his weakened left leg. His free hand fisted around the hog chain to steady himself. But he rested only a moment, in the icy spray of river water thrown up by the paddles, before he started to clamber up on to the Boiler Deck.

'He's aboard,' Charity reported as Henry's three victims emerged from the crowd on the wharf to shake their fists and rant at the departing boat. 'Do you think he'll be clapped in irons or something?'

When she turned, she saw that Edge was unbuttoning his

coat. Sunlight glinted on the bullets slotted into his gunbelt loops.

'Maybe not, if he stole enough to pay for a ticket.'

'Are you going to cause trouble because of what happened in town?' Her pretty face was creased by an anxious frown.

On the wharf the crowd dispersed, except for a small group gathered around the unconscious stevedore. Aboard the *Delta Dawn,* trembling and shuddering against a mid-river current, the crew resumed their duties and most of the passengers hurried to find shelter in the salon from the cutting cold of the slipstream.

'Make it a habit to be ready for trouble, ma'am,' Edge told her as the Hurricane Deck became deserted except for the woman and himself.

'He's hardly likely to start any, Mr Edge. He's bound to pretend he doesn't recognise us.'

The half-breed shook his head. 'Ain't nothing certain about life. Except death.'

Charity shivered, perhaps from the cold. Edge took her arm and steered her off the open deck and along the railed companionway which ran past the doors to private compartments and public cabins. She made to halt at the doorway of her quarters, but the pressure of Edge's grip kept her moving.

'I need to eat,' he told her. 'How about you?'

She glanced at him sharply. 'I wasn't going to invite you inside, if that's what you think!'

'Only thought in my mind right now concerns food.' He smiled. 'I'm buying.'

'Not simply for the sake of watching me eat, I think?' she countered lightly.

As they neared the door to the dining salon, the late-boarding and unexpected passenger was hustled across the Boiler Deck by the uniformed Master's Mate and a roustabout. Henry was limping badly again, but was neither breathless nor anxious as he was escorted to the stairway which led up to the wheel-house. He smiled at Charity and the expression remained in place when his gaze shifted to Edge. Then, for part of a second, a sneer altered his mouthline and his eyes showed fleeting surprise. But he recovered quickly.

With both arms held by his captors, he was unable to touch the brim of his new hat. But he inclined his head. 'Good afternoon,' he greeted pleasantly.

Charity refused to look at him or respond. Edge worked

some saliva into his mouth and spat it forcefully out over the rail into the river.

'After a morning best forgotten, feller,' the half-breed answered evenly. He locked his narrow-eyed gaze on the face of the prisoner for a moment, trying to recall where he had seen the man before the hold-up. But the memory stayed securely locked in the back of his mind.

Henry nodded his head again, but this time in acknowledgement, as he was urged up the stairway. 'Some you win and some you lose,' he called back over his shoulder. 'I'm not one to bear grudges.'

'But you are one, sure enough,' Edge muttered.

Henry had been hurried to the top of the stairway, out of earshot.

'Meaning he is a pervert, Mr Edge,' Charity said, waiting for the half-breed to open the dining-salon door for her.

'Your word, not mine.' He did what was expected of him, but she hesitated on the threshold.

'I want your word, Mr Edge,' she said earnestly.

'I got a lot, ma'am. Fruit, queer, homosexual – '

She cut him off with a shake of her head. 'Your word that if I allow you to buy my lunch for me, you will not look upon it as a debt I owe.'

'No sweat. Buy your own grub.'

She blushed yet again. 'You mean you would expect repayment by . . . with me . . . payment in kind?'

'When I feed a horse, ma'am, it's to keep him fit for riding.'

Charity made a spluttering sound, spun on her heels and retreated along the companionway towards her cabin. 'I am not a horse, Mr Edge!' she flung back at him.

Edge shrugged and eyed her rigid back and swaying hips ruefully. 'That's no reason not to like your oats, ma'am,' he responded.

CHAPTER THREE

Edge ate a boiled beef lunch alone and when he was drinking his coffee afterwards, Henry appeared in the dining salon. The thin, pale-faced man was no longer a prisoner and his gaunt features were wreathed in a relaxed smile. As he came in and sat down at a vacant table on the far side of the salon from Edge, there was a break in many conversations and an atmosphere of disapproval was evident in the near silence.

'Those people on the dock owed me money,' he said to the coloured steward who approached his table – speaking loud enough for everyone in the salon to hear. 'The master of this tub believed me. What others think doesn't overly concern me.'

'I just serve the passengers, sir!' the steward answered, his eyes big and round. Then he laughed. 'If I got paid to think, sir, I'd be in the poorhouse for sure.'

Many conversations restarted, to contribute to a steady buzz of noise. Henry concentrated on ordering his meal and then eating it. Having made his point, he showed no further interest in his fellow passengers: until Horace Ferris entered to have his lunch. It was obvious that Henry recognised Ferris, but the short, fat man was still preoccupied with secret anxieties and paid no attention to his surroundings or its inhabitants.

As the half-breed rose to leave, he sensed eyes directing more than mild interest towards his back. At the door, he cast a fast glance across the salon: and both Ferris and Henry were part of a second late in snapping their heads around to pretend total absorption in what was on their plates. In that sliver of time, Edge saw hatred in the dark eyes of Henry and something akin to regret on the flabby face of the older man.

He went below then, to the midships cargo hold. A dozen passengers had already claimed sleeping space, in areas not already staked by the roustabouts for their rest periods. There was a mixture of the sexes across an age span from childhood to old age. The sole common denominator which grouped hold passengers and roustabouts together was poverty. It showed in the meagre food they ate from waxpaper packages, in their clothing and even in their faces. There were two Chinese among the passengers and a Negro roustabout. All the rest were white.

Edge's entrance was viewed by all with idle curiosity. But, after he had taken a stinking straw mattress and two heavily stained blankets from a communal pile and spread the bedding on a clear area of decking, the sparse interest waned.

There was no stove and a large sign warned against the dangers of smoking close to inflammable cargo. Whatever was packed in the crates tightly stacked across two thirds of the hold space smelled musty. But, as he sprawled out under the blankets, his hat over his face, Edge soon became aware of a more powerful stink: despite the bitter cold, the odour of unwashed bodies was strong.

The *Delta Dawn* made good time throughout the afternoon and evening, steaming at a steady speed on a broad river under a clear sky. The current was constantly against her but the engines continued to thud rhythmically, drawing power from the forward boilers and turning the paddle-wheel at a regular two hundred dips a minute. The river level was high after the blizzard of the morning and it was only infrequently that the pilot had to order a change of course to avoid sand-bars and timber snags.

The putrid air of the confined hold did not bother Edge and neither did the juddering of the decking and thump of the engine. When the best of anything was available and he could afford it, he enjoyed it; when the worst was unavoidable, he endured it – his mood of the moment unaffected by outside influences.

As he slept beneath his hat and the blankets, his mind triggered dreams which he would not recall when he awoke. His contentment of the morning was gone now: a short-lived sense of well-being that was created when he awoke in his hotel room and did not feel pain in his wrenched ankle and bullet-creased arm: both injuries unwanted bonuses for the job which brought him from San Francisco to Omaha.

Hanging on the wall opposite the foot of his bed had been a print of the waterfront at Bismarck: and, feeling the drifter's urge to move on, he had decided to head for the bleak-looking town in the wilderness of the northern Dakotas.

31

It was a territory which held as many memories as Iowa for him: of good times and bad. All of them centred upon a woman named Beth who had changed her name from Day to Hedges. A woman and a marriage: holding out a promise that the future for Edge could be better than the best there had been in the distant past.

But a raiding party of Sioux Indians caused the promise to be violently broken. For Beth died, more horribly than Jamie had met his end and, by a cruel twist of brutal fate, in a manner that placed the onus of her death upon a husband who loved her more dearly than he had ever loved anything or anybody.

He dreamed of Beth as he slept through the afternoon and early evening, the level of his sleep just below waking: not consciously aware of his surroundings but certain of his capability to be roused with total recall should danger threaten. Another skill developed, or talent honed, by the lessons of war.

Although she looked not at all like Beth, perhaps it was his meeting with Charity Meagher which had sown the seeds in his mind which germinated into the dreams. Or maybe it was the fact that he was aboard a stern wheeler thrashing northwards towards the Dakotas. Bismarck was a long way east and north of the Black Hills where he had sought to put down roots with his wife. But it was in the same harsh territory.

His sleeping mind flitted to another time and another place. The Big Bend of the Rio Grande where, amid violence and death, he had met another woman. Also unlike Beth, but long enough after the passing of his wife for him to feel the need of another woman. But he lost her, too, as irrevocably as if death had claimed her. And the ten thousand dollars she paid him seemed to hold out a fresh hope and a new promise to fill the bleak future with something good.

But the money was taken from him. Destroyed, just as an earlier ten thousand dollars had been destroyed – that time south of the border in Mexico before he even laid hands upon it.

His dreaming had gone out of chronological sequence now. Mexico had been long ago. After Jamie, but before Beth. There had been blood and shattered bodies. But then these elements were almost always present. Except for brief periods – such as his time in Omaha until this morning. And a man like Edge could feel good in such a spell of peace amid an existence that attracted violence. Even though he knew, without being aware of how he knew, that the good would end and evil would close in on him again.

'You're a troubled man, I'd say.'

Edge was already awake and had tipped his hat back on to his head as he folded up from the stinking mattress. The Negro roustabout was sitting on an upended pail four feet away. He was smoking a rough-carved pipe and held the stem clenched tight between his teeth as he spoke. And he did not make the comment until the half-breed was sitting upright.

'I talk in my sleep?' Edge asked, glancing at the black. He was about twenty-five, tall, broad and solidly built. He had proud, handsome features, given a quality of toughness by a two-day growth of bristles. He was warmly dressed in an old, thick coat and all his hair was trapped under a skull-tight wool hat.

'Don't hardly breathe, mister. And don't move a muscle. Sure don't move your hand offen that holstered gun. Only a man with a troubled mind sleeps with a grip on his gun.'

'You an expert, feller?' Edge asked, and looked around the hold. There were no lamps but moonlight streamed in with the bitterly cold air from the glassless portholes. There were perhaps thirty passengers cramping the quarters now. Most of them bedded down in family groups. Four men played poker for dead matchsticks. All the off-duty crewmen except the Negro were asleep.

'I'm black in a white man's world, mister. Makes me a real expert on trouble and handlin' it so I don't get hurt – much.'

Edge eased to his feet, stooped to cover the mattress with the blanket and stretched the final remnants of rest from his limbs as he straightened. 'You just talking, feller? Or you saying something?'

The Negro shrugged and grinned around his pipe. 'If I'm sayin' somethin', mister, I reckon I ain't tellin' you nothin' new.' Then he moved the pipe and looked morosely into its empty bowl. 'But that holdin' of the gun while you sleep, that's easy to see. There's an air of death hangin' around you, mister. I'm the seventh son of a seventh son and that means I got a feelin' for such things.'

'Means something else, too,' the half-breed muttered as he turned to head for the stairway to the hatch.

'What's that, mister?'

'Both your pa and his pa had a feeling for something.'

The Negro laughed with genuine humour. 'Ain't never been

3   33

much else poor folk ever could do after the day's work was done, mister!' he called.

'Shut your loud mouth, Linn!' a roused roustabout snarled sourly. 'Some folks need to sleep nights!'

Linn's coat reached to his ankles as he squatted on the up-turned pail. He pulled one flap aside to show a knife sheath strapped to the outside of his left pants leg. With smooth skill, he slid out the blade and sent it spinning across the hold. It was an underarm throw, with just a short swing of the arm. But easy strength powered the weapon with a speed that almost deceived the eye. The point of the knife was buried an inch into a bulkhead – no greater distance above the bulbous belly of the man who had complained.

'And some don't, you Irish lard-barrel!' the Negro hissed with soft venom. He flipped open the other side of his coat and prepared to draw another knife from a similar sheath. But the fat Irishman made no counter move.

'It's called insomnia,' Edge said from the head of the stairs.

'What's that?' Linn asked, grinning again.

'What runs in your family, feller.'

The Negro laughed loud again, but this time there were no complaints.

Edge stepped out on to the Main Deck and immediately felt much colder. Below in the hold the presence of so many people had served to raise the otherwise unheated atmosphere a few degrees. Outside, the air through which the *Delta Dawn* was pushing had an icy bite that put a stiffness into exposed skin and found its way through clothing to raise goose bumps.

Overhead, the sky was bright with the moon and myriad glinting stars. Smoke from the forward-mounted stacks curled down and skimmed off the roof of the wheel-house before disintegrating behind the boat. Sparks hissed as they touched dew on the point of freezing. Thin ice floes were shattered by the bow and the surviving shards of ice were sucked into the path of the paddle-wheel and turned to white water again before being hurled out into the wash.

The engines were having to draw more power from the glowing boilers to maintain the same speed through the strengthening downriver currents of the Missouri.

Nebraska, on one side of the river and Iowa on the other looked dark and foreboding despite the brightness of the three-quarter moon.

But Edge spent no time in contemplation of the night. He

34

merely looked at it and even smelt it as he moved forward towards the stairway which gave access to the upper decks. Trusting his senses to warn him of potential danger. But he was alone in the open, coat collar turned high and hat brim pulled low.

The biting air was static, only the forward thrust of the *Delta Dawn* giving it an illusion of tugging him. It felt less harsh when he had reached the Hurricane Deck and started towards the stern along the companionway in front of the port cabins. For his back was towards the chilling assault.

There were running lights at the top of the bow spars and a dim glow of lamplight from the wheel-house. A strip of yellow at the glass transom above the door to Charity Meagher's cabin went out as Edge drew near. Then the door folded inwards and the woman stepped across the threshold.

'Oh!' she said, too dramatically, as the half-breed halted before he bumped into her. And the moonlight made it unnecessary for her to look at him quite so hard before admitting to recognition. 'It's you, Mr Edge.'

'You want to pinch me to make sure?' he asked lightly.

She was wearing the same coat as earlier, but now it was merely draped, cloak fashion, over her shoulders. She held it in place at her throat with one hand, but it gaped lower down to show a blue dress trimmed with white lace: tight to the waist then flaring over many petticoats to her ankles. She seemed on the point of a stern retort, but then changed her mind.

'May we start again? On the understanding that there are no strings attached?' She smiled tentatively, blushed, and looked down at the deck. 'I'm the kind of girl that does not like to be rushed. Is it a deal?'

She looked up now, to show him her face instead of the crown of her head. Incredibly, despite the icy slipstream of the churning boat, her flushed face was sheened with nervous perspiration.

'You just made the deal, ma'am,' Edge told her with a quiet grin as he took her arm. 'And we both know I'm going to get the pot. Just the matter of when you show me what I have to top.'

She said, 'Oh!' again, but with genuine shock this time. However, she allowed him to steer her sedately along the companionway and into the dining salon.

Most passengers who could afford the price of a served meal

35

had already eaten and the majority of the tables had been stripped of their starched white coverings. Many were left bare and it was at these that individuals or groups of men and a few women sat drinking: supplied with beer and hard liquor by stewards who moved back and forth between a well-stocked bar in an alcove.

Three tables were draped with green baize and at these a trio of poker games were underway. Four more were still set for eating and it was at one of these that Edge and Charity sat down. The brunette, her colour returned to its normal light tan, was genuinely surprised again – when Edge held her chair and took her coat.

'You haven't always been a . . . '

She either could not think of a suitable word, or felt the word might insult him. So she let the sentence hang and showed him the top of her head again as he gave the coats and his hat to a steward and accepted a menu in exchange.

'I've been a lot of things in a lot of places, ma'am,' he answered. 'Don't ever excuse what I am the time I am it.'

He showed her the menu and they both ordered T-bone steaks with deep-fried potatoes and side salads. The prices were high.

Charity seemed grateful the half-breed had not been insulted by the implication of her remark. 'Because you never make mistakes in anything you do, or are?'

Edge shifted his gaze back and forth across the room, recalling her earlier mild triumph when she had been able to correct his preconceived notion of how she had obtained a cabin on the *Delta Dawn*. 'I ain't God, ma'am,' he answered.

There was a smell of cooking in the salon, strengthening and fading as the swing door to the galley opened and closed. It was mixed in with the other odours of fresh and stale liquor, old and new tobacco smoke and the wood burning in the heating stove. The noise was low-key: voices in many conversations, cutlery on crockery, bottle necks against glasses and silver dollars chinking on beds of paper money. Behind the sounds created in the salon was the throb of the engines, the thrash of the paddle-wheel and the trickle of water along the boat's hull.

'But you never apologise?' Charity insisted. 'Just as God does not – for all the suffering He allows to take place on His earth.'

Horace Ferris and Henry were in on one of the poker

games. Sharing a table with a short, young, weasel-faced man in Western garb and a thin, middle-aged man attired in similar city clothes to Ferris. In the stove-heated atmosphere of the salon, Henry had taken off his topcoat and suit jacket to display a fancy red and green vest with a gold watch chain slung between two pockets. His shirt sleeves were rolled up and his discarded clothes were hung on a coatstand behind him.

'He may allow it, ma'am. But He don't cause it. Why should He apologise?'

Edge had completed his survey – taking in more detail than when he had glanced around the salon on first entering. Now he looked at the woman seated opposite him, certain that of the other passengers, only Ferris and Henry had more than a passing interest in him. And that, at the moment, took second place to the cards they were being dealt by the middle-aged, distinguished looking player.

'People are their own masters, is that it?' Charity asked rhetorically. 'They take their own actions and must be responsible for them.'

'Unless they get paid to take orders.' He smiled bleakly. 'Without tying the string that says they do things their way.'

The gaze from his ice-blue eyes was frank. First he looked into her face and saw that, in artificial light it was only fractionally less attractive than under always flattering moonglow. Then he shifted his gaze to briefly study the contours of her shoulders, breasts and midriff: the firm curves and angles of her body tightly hugged by the high-necked dress.

'And what about when you get hurt yourself by your own actions, Mr Edge? Is there never self-apology? Regret? Remorse? Or even self-denigration?'

She spoke quickly now, not enjoying the cold-eyed stare that seemed capable of looking through her dress and underwear to see the sweat-tacky flesh beneath.

Then the steward delivered their food, leaning between them to hide her embarrassment and block the half-breed's unemotional eyes.

'Like crying for my Ma if she wasn't around when I hurt myself, I grew out of all that, ma'am. Took longer and the learning was harder is all.'

She watched him eat before starting herself. And again was pleasantly surprised at his discreet, unselfconscious table manners.

'You've done a lot of long and hard learning, haven't you,

Mr Edge?' she said at length, when the half-breed made no attempt to restart a conversation. 'Some in school rooms but far more outside.'

The salon was becoming more crowded, most of the passengers intent upon using its facilities as a bar room. One more poker game started.

'Men and women are animals, ma'am. Just able to learn more than most, is all. How much they learn and what they decide to forget is up to them.'

He ate fast because he was hungry. The food was not good, but it was filling. Whether or not he had once been used to better, Charity Meagher was unable to tell. The conclusion she did reach was that the man across the table from her probably regarded food like most other things in life. If he needed to eat, he ate.

And, as she picked daintily at the food on her own plate, she discovered a shameful excitement rising from the pit of her stomach. For it was obvious Edge felt the need of a woman. Would this desire be appeased in the same manner he satisfied his hunger for food? Or could a woman arouse passion – perhaps even tenderness – in a man whose appetites for all things seemed to be so jaded.

She felt her flesh become hot as she considered the challenge: no longer lying to herself. Not *a* woman: but herself. She had hinted – if not promised – that he could share her bed. It had never been of her own free will and she had hoped she could avoid it. But now, in the over-heated salon, she realised she welcomed the opportunity: both aroused and frightened by the challenge.

'You've either got hot blood or a fire in your belly, ma'am,' Edge said, as he rattled his knife and fork down on to his empty plate.

Charity realised the heat she felt from within her had suffused her face with a blush again. She started, and knocked over a glass of water.

'I'm ready when you are,' he added.

She had to swallow hard a piece of steak that needed chewing. Then she choked on it and drank gratefully from Edge's glass.

'You are the most direct and to the point person I have ever met in my life!' she accused hoarsely. 'You're making me feel like a ... a ... who ... a dancehall girl.'

'Never have dealt with that kind, ma'am,' Edge told her as

38

he pushed back his chair and dropped a five-dollar bill on the table.

'And I have never been in this situation with a man whose first name I didn't know before!' she retorted.

But she pushed back her chair and stood up.

'Never form an opinion about something before you've tried it, ma'am,' the half-breed told her, holding out her coat.

'At least call me Charity,' she said stiffly. 'And I would like to know your name.'

Another voice spoke – loud and angry – before Edge could comply. 'You, sir, are a cheat!'

The accusation cut across every other sound in the salon and silenced it.

'Was born Josiah Hedges,' the half-breed supplied, then joined everyone else in looking towards the source of gathering trouble.

It was the tall, thin man with a stamp of distinction who had shouted. He sat rigid in his chair, but the sparse flesh of his cheeks quivered as he glowered across the table at Ferris. The shorter man had his back to Edge and Charity so they could see nothing of his reaction except the fact that the nape of his neck, below his greying hair, was bright red – and that he was as unmoving as his accuser. The youngster with the weasel-like features looked frightened and had his hands pushed against the table-top, as if he was preparing to lunge up and run. Henry was staring hard at Edge, an expression of surprised fascination on his weakly handsome face.

'You have pre-empted me with a lie, sir!' Horace Ferris said, his voice slow and controlled; the manner of his speech emphasising its Deep South drawl. 'The boot, I feel, is on the other foot.'

'Please, no!' Charity gasped, clutching at her throat with both hands.

The door from the companionway swung open and two uniformed officers came in: the master and the mate, for a moment wearing expressions of forced pleasure since they considered the necessity to mingle with passengers one of their most onerous duties. But, even before the cold air which streamed inside with them had started to cool the stove heat of the salon, they had sensed trouble and spotted its source.

'You again, Rhett!' the master of the *Delta Dawn* snarled.

He was a big man – standing taller than six feet with a great deal of fat layered on a frame that obviously commanded considerable strength. He rolled like an ocean-going seaman when he moved. His mate was smaller, thinner and faster, but from nervousness or deference stayed behind his superior officer. He had a Frontier Colt stuck under his belt at the middle of his belly. He fisted a hand around the butt and cocked the gun, but did not draw it.

Edge received just these fleeting impressions of the men as he glanced towards the sudden draught of cold air. But then, his eyes narrowing to the merest slits and his lips curling back in a hard, humourless grin of satisfaction, he flicked his attention back towards the poker table on the far side of the salon.

It wasn't Henry Rhett who had been hovering tantalisingly on the brink of his memory. It was merely his looks which had caused a mental drape to sway. The voicing of his full name wrenched the drape aside.

Rhett grinned, seeing that Edge had reacted to his name – in a different manner but just as emphatically – as he, himself, had responded to the half-breed's more quietly spoken revelation of a few seconds earlier.

The distinguished looking man powered erect then, delving a hand inside his suit jacket.

A woman screamed.

The weasel-faced youngster chose to go backwards instead of up, lifting his feet from the floor and shoving hard against the table. His chair tipped and he gathered himself into a ball as the back crashed to the floor and he threw himself into a bone-jarring roll.

Rhett reached behind, a long arm snaking towards his hanging coats.

Ferris also remained seated, but his shoulder blades rippled the back of his coat as he did something fast with his hands.

Charity squealed, in both alarm and pain, as Edge hooked a hand over each of her shoulders and pushed her down hard on to her haunches: where she unbalanced and slammed on to her rump.

All over the salon, passengers and stewards sought the relative safety of the deck floor.

'Gentlemen!' the rolling and swaying master yelled, his tone midway between a plea and an order.

The mate drew his Colt but did not raise the gun.

The accuser of Ferris drew a tiny brass-framed Darling pepperbox: and his scowl of injured pride became a snarl of triumph. But then Ferris lunged up from his chair, his hands

40

hooked under the table to lift and throw it forward.

Charity started to get up, anxious eyes seeking to watch events. Edge raised a foot and rested it gently against the top of her spine. Then he shoved forcefully and the woman's cry was entirely of pain as she sprawled out on to her belly and her chin cracked against the decking.

The half-breed's cold glower was enough to keep her flat to the floor when she wrenched her head around to glare at him.

He stepped to the side, wide of the line of fire from the multi-barrel weapon.

But the pepperbox wavered in its aim as the man holding it was forced backwards by the tipping table.

'Hold it, mister!' the master bellowed. 'Wren!'

The senior officer skidded to a halt and leaned to the side, shooting out an arm to point towards the disrupted card game. His mate snapped up the Colt, swinging it between Ferris and the other man.

Ferris's right hand came out from under his jacket, thumb and forefinger holding the point of a knife blade.

From his new position, Edge caught a glimpse of Ferris's profile. The face was stark white, in contrast to the crimson hue at the nape of his neck. And, etched deep into the face, were the lines of naked fear. For the New Orleans business-man realised he had wasted time by tipping the table – that he could not throw the knife before the ring trigger of the Darling exploded a killing shot into his heart.

'You're covered, damnit!' the *Delta Dawn*'s master roared.

He was about to follow this with a threat – or perhaps an order to the confused mate.

But a gunshot exploded, the stink of burnt powder merged with the odour of burnt fabric.

A small hole appeared in the centre of the forehead of the man holding the pepperbox. For an instant, he remained erect, his look of triumph changed to one of surprise. Then the killing bullet crashed out through the top of his skull, trailed by a torrent of liquid red. The glaze of death dropped over his eyes and his skin texture abruptly looked much older. He took an involuntary step backwards, then crumpled: limp and loose, as if death had melted his bones.

Henry Rhett, who had seemed to rock backwards in his chair to stay clear of the line of fire, now straightened, taking his hand out from under his hanging jacket. The hand was empty. A final whisp of smoke rose from the jacket, where

41

the revolver action of his combination weapon had blasted a hole through the material.

'It was the dead man that was cheating, Captain McBride,' Rhett said easily, looking odd and somehow vulnerable as he sat in the chair beside the overturned table. 'And you know I know my business.'

People got tentatively to their feet: some remaining erect and others dropping gratefully into chairs.

'I didn't see nothin'!' the weasel-faced young man said hurriedly as he came upright, massaging the bruises of his self-inflicted fall. 'Didn't see nobody do nothin'.'

Charity Meagher started to rise, wincing as the injuries of her enforced tumble protested with stabs of pain. She glared in anger at Edge again as he approached her. But then sighed with relief as he helped her to her feet and demonstrated that he could use his easy strength with gentleness.

'Mr Wren!'

'Sir!'

'Escort all three men to my quarters! And arrange for the cadaver to be removed!'

Wren made a jerking gesture with his Colt. Ferris, looking both afraid and ashamed, complied first. Then the youngest of the trio followed, still muttering that he knew nothing of what had happened. Rhett took his time, shrugging into his jacket and topcoat before heading for the door.

'It's all over now, ladies and gentlemen!' McBride announced, attempting a placating attitude. 'I'd like to apologise to you for what happened. And assure you it won't occur again. So you just go on enjoying yourselves the way you were before the incident. Steward, drinks on the line for the rest of tonight.'

The master had a round, ruddy face with a pitted skin, an untidy moustache and dark eyes that looked incapable of sincerity.

'Thank you,' Charity said with a sigh, continuing to lean against the half-breed. 'I could have been killed and you did the right thing.'

Edge knew she was talking in an effort to conceal the concerned exchange of glances between herself and Horace Ferris.

'Most of the time I do,' he responded absently as Ferris pulled open the door and admitted a new draught of icy air to dispel the last traces of gunshot odour from the salon.

Ferris went out and the youngster was hard on his heels.

Henry Rhett halted in front of Edge, aware of but ignoring the Colt of Wren aimed at his back.

'Captain Hedges who served with the Union cavalry during the war?'

Edge nodded, his impassive eyes studying Rhett up close for the first time. Henry was a year or so older than his brother would have been – had he lived. As tall and lean, but with a suggestion of latent strength that Bob had never displayed: probably had never possessed. Now that the family connection was established, the facial resemblance between the two brothers was striking. The same shade of blue in the eyes, the same high forehead, the same slightly sunken cheeks and the same fault in the structure of the mouth and jaw that robbed the whole of manly handsomeness. For the line of the lower half of the face was weak, due to the simpering pout that the lips formed in repose and the too-perfect symmetry of the chin.

But, whereas this had been a physical mark of Bob Rhett's craven cowardice, the surviving brother had already demonstrated his ability to control fear in a crisis. Another difference between Henry and Bob was that the elder brother was not so blatantly homosexual as the younger had been.

'I heard a lot about you from Bob,' Rhett said. 'He thought a great deal of you.'

'He thought a great deal about all men,' the half-breed muttered as passengers yelled orders for free drinks, eager to take advantage of McBride's offer.

'We can't help the way we are,' Rhett answered simply, and merely grimaced when the muzzle of the mate's gun was shoved into the small of his back.

'Move, Henry,' Wren ordered.

Rhett ignored him. 'Bob wrote me you didn't try to make his life hell like some of the other guys in the outfit – just because he wasn't like them.'

'Sure didn't hold it against him,' the half-breed growled.

Rhett grinned. 'Rib all you like, Captain. Bob could take it and so can I.'

'Move it!' Wren snarled, responding to a glare from Mc-Bride. 'Or I'm in lousy trouble, too.'

'See you, Captain,' Henry said evenly. 'But I won't be looking to kill you for what happened to my friend this morning.' He started forward and glanced back over his shoulder. 'So

43

you can relax and enjoy yourself. No sweat, okay?'

'Intend to, feller,' the half-breed replied, and looked meaningfully at Charity as Rhett was escorted out through the doorway.

The woman had completely recovered her composure now and was eyeing Edge with pensive concentration, behind which was surprise.

'His brother served under you during the war?'

The half-breed smiled with his mouth. 'In one way,' he allowed, and gripped her upper arm more firmly to steer her through the doorway. 'You ready to try the other?'

CHAPTER FOUR

Charity Meagher was afraid of accepting the challenge. Her trembling as the tall, lean, taciturn man guided her towards her cabin was not at all due to the intense cold of the moon and star bright night. He was big and he was strong and the constant look in his narrow eyes and the line of his mouth more than merely hinted at the cruelty that was held on a tight leash just beneath the surface of his being.

Her hand shook too much as she tried to fit the key into the door lock. He took it from her gently, but this gesture – and the politeness he showed in ushering her ahead of him into the cabin – seemed insignificant. Her mind refused to acknowledge his gentlemanly conduct at the dining table. She remembered only the casual way in which he had killed a man that morning, his bitter retort when she asked about his past, the power of his hands pushing her to the floor and the brutal way he kicked her down again when she tried to rise.

His actions at the shipping company office had been for the good of all the victims of the hold-up. He perhaps had a good reason for not wishing to discuss his marriage. And the force he used in the dining salon had been to protect Charity.

But, as he closed the cabin door and leaned against it, she found she could think only evil of him. At the hold-up, he had put many lives in danger for purely selfish reasons. Did he refuse to talk of his wife because he had killed her? He protected her in the dining salon simply because he was lusting for a woman.

'I'd rather not have the lamp lit,' Charity said huskily.

'Your place, you make the rules,' Edge replied as he took off his hat. 'I'll let you know if I've got any objections.'

There was no lust in his voice. No passion. No gentleness. No nothing. As Charity went to the double bed and dropped her coat over a nearby chair, she thought fleetingly of the way he ate his food – indifferently, disinterestedly, impassively. But

45

the recollection did not restimulate the hot anticipation she had experienced in the crowded salon. For now she was alone with him, in a confined space dominated by her body, his presence and a bed.

He had taken off his coat now, and dropped it to the floor. He let his hat fall on top of it and then began to unbutton his shirt. The cabin's sole porthole was blinded by a drape, but moonlight was filtered and dim as it shone through the frosted glass transom above the door. Enough for her to see him – and for him to see her.

He eased his shirt out from under his pants and shrugged out of it. There was dark hair on his chest, but less than she had expected. The skin of his torso was only a shade lighter than his facial complexion. It was stretched taut over solid, muscular flesh, rippling slightly when he moved. Livid scar tissue showed at his left shoulder and right hip. There was a much fresher wound just below the elbow joint on the inside of his left arm. He unbuckled his gunbelt and dropped it on the pile of clothing. Then the belt beneath, and started on the front fastening of his pants.

'You're making the rules until I get my pants off, Charity,' he said softly, speaking her given name for the first time. 'So you better start stripping of your own accord. For me, it's been a long time since the last time.'

She made several nervous sounds in her throat before she could voice her words. 'The last time for me was the only time.' The moonlight through the frosted glass caused the teardrops to glisten on her cheeks. 'He wasn't like you at all. And I loved him. I'm scared, Edge.'

His voice was abruptly harsh, as he advanced on her, still wearing his kerchief over the razor pouch and beaded thong, and his pants and boots. 'What do you think I am, lady?' he snarled. 'A frigging horny bobcat on the prowl for any damn she that smells like it's ready for rut?'

She vented a low howl and stepped back, so that her legs banged against the side of the bed. She heard the half-breed's arm travel through the air, rather than saw it. But she felt the stinging impact of the back of his hand slam into her tear moist cheek. The howl reached the shrill pitch of a scream of pain then, as she was flung backwards across the bed. But the sound was short-lived: its ending trapped in her throat as he knelt one knee on the bed beside her and clapped the damaging hand over her gaping mouth.

He lowered his face down towards her own, his eyes as narrow as hers were wide: his breath as hot against her ear as she knew hers was against his palm.

'I came here expecting to screw you, Miss Charity Meagher,' he said, his voice soft, each word spurting more hot air into her ear. 'Because I figured you were hot to get screwed. If you are, strip your own threads off. If you ain't, I'll belt you in the mouth again and get the hell out of here. On the other hand, if you're the kind that likes to get took the hard way, I'll just leave. I ain't that kind and you made a mistake. Just like we all do from time to time.'

He released his grip on her and stood up. She had been holding her breath while she was trapped and now she remained across the bed as she exhaled and inhaled several times.

'I'm sorry, Edge,' she said, struggling to sit up. 'But you can't expect everyone to be the same as – '

'It's the difference that adds the spice, lady,' he growled. 'You gonna put out or do I pull out?'

Her dress had a back fastening. When she raised her hands to the nape of her neck, the movement jutted her breasts more aggressively.

Edge turned his back on her and went to the door, where he stripped off the rest of his clothing. He had never pretended to himself that he was superhuman: was just aware that he commanded a higher than average degree of self-control – most importantly when his survival was at risk. Now, as he listened to the rustle of fabric against flesh and to the sounds of a woman breathing, his life was not in danger. But his pride in the almost as important matter of sexual prowess was.

Beth had been the last woman he took. At the start of the war, he had surrendered that part of his innocence to a girl named Jeannie Fisher. When every shred of every aspect of innocence had been ripped from him by war, there had been rape.

All of these a long time ago and far from here: where a new woman was preparing to open her body to him. And, because there had been so many nights of single-bed sleeping since then, Edge recognised the danger of watching Charity undress – and welcomed the biting chill of the unheated air that helped to keep the inner fire burning low until the moment for flaring passion arrived.

Footfalls sounded on the companionway outside the cabin

47

doorway. And voices talked softly. Without hearing the words distinctly, Edge recognised the tones of Ferris's Deep South drawl and the almost musical accent of Henry Rhett, caught somewhere between the nasal New England speech of his up-bringing and a mixture of strains picked up on wide travels. The door to the next cabin opened and closed. The bedsprings behind Edge creaked.

'I was going to point out that you can't expect everybody to be the same as you,' Charity said, a little dejectedly. 'Some people – especially women – have a more romantic view of life than you. Not least this aspect of life.'

Edge turned, and vented a low grunt of satisfaction that she was under the covers: the blankets bulky enough to do no more than hint at the contours of her body beneath. But he felt his arousal again, as he approached the bed and saw that the woman's eyes, in contrast to her voice, expressed excite-ment.

They ranged a gaze over his body and face with almost as much arrogance as he had surveyed her at the dining table.

'Women talk a lot about romance,' he answered, his voice involuntarily husky, as he lifted the covers and slid his lean frame into the bed. 'But comes a time for even them when the talking has to stop. Wouldn't you say the time's come for action?'

She was on her back, her body moist with the sweat of wanting. She trembled at the contact of his cold flesh. Then tremored with excitement as his words breathed hot air into her ear, one of his hands found the firm, large mound of a breast and the other explored through the secret tangle of soft hair to probe the musky wetness of her centre.

'Oh!' she breathed, spreading her legs and digging the nails of her hand into the small of his back.

'That don't count, I figure,' Edge murmured, submitting to the demand of her clawed hand and easing himself on to her spread-eagled body.

She writhed beneath him, raising her legs to encircle him. As one hand became even more like a talon on his back, the other snaked between flesh to grasp him and direct the initial thrust into her. His own hands kneaded her breasts with mounting fierceness as his hungry lips sucked at the side of her throat.

For the first time, he smelt the perfume in her hair.

48

The engines of the *Delta Dawn* pounded in a measured cadence of easy power.

Charity's hands moved from his back to his head, her nails clawing at his flesh to erupt blood which mixed with the sweat. She forced his face closer to her neck. Then her hands went down and beneath herself, to press at her buttocks, as if trying to arch her body to meet his thrusting want. She groaned and threw her head from side to side, the movement in time with the probe and retraction of the maleness inside her. Sweat ran from both bodies and mingled.

The action of the coupling man and woman caught up with the speed of the engines' throb, kept pace for a few moments, then passed it.

'Oh, my sweet . . . !' Charity groaned.

Edge felt a burning wetness engulf the centre of his desire as the woman climaxed and a split-second later his own lust was expended in urgent spasms towards her womb.

They clung tight to each other for stretched seconds, until the effects of their draining spread to every part of their bodies. Then, as Charity sighed, Edge eased out of her and off her: to lie on his back beside her.

'Thank you, Edge,' the woman said after seconds had elapsed, with just the sounds of the engines and water along the hull to disturb the stillness. She caught her breath.

'It wasn't no favour,' the half-breed muttered.

'Let a body finish, please. You had a wife once. And I guess there have been a lot of other women. I don't care about them. I don't care how you were with them. What was bad with me was my fault. Before. I just want to thank you for thinking of me. John never did.'

Edge swung his bare feet to the floor, rose from the bed and padded across to where his clothes were heaped by the door.

'But I figure he was strong on the romancing bit, uh?'

'Because he really did love me, Edge. You don't mind me calling you Edge? You've had that name a long time, haven't you? People grow into their names. I think you've grown out of the one you had.'

'Edge is fine.'

'He surely is,' Charity murmured, and stretched her arms, relishing the luxury of the warmth and space in the bed now she had it to herself. Then her face became earnest, and her voice matched it. 'I don't want an apology from you for hitting me. I deserved it. You don't want me to say I'm sorry for deserving it, do you?'

'Talking time again?' Edge asked as he dressed hurriedly, experiencing the discomfort of the cold now, and the vulnerability of nakedness.

'Not if you don't want to. But you're welcome to stay in this compartment, Edge. You may make the rules and I know I can make no demands.'

'Obliged, Charity,' he responded, fully dressed now except for his topcoat, hat and gunbelt. 'I'll be back.'

'Where are you going?' she asked, suddenly anxious – not wanting to lose something she had accepted with reluctance but now needed to keep.

He had on the gunbelt and hat and coat now. Because she could not see his face clearly in the moonshadow of his hatbrim, the grin he showed seemed to express a great deal of humour. 'What you just had has another use. And when a man's gotta go, a man's gotta go.'

'Oh,' she said, and wriggled down in the bed to hide her face from him.

Edge stepped outside and turned towards the stern. The time was now beyond midnight and the only lights on the *Delta Dawn* glowed bright at the top of the spars and dimly from the windows of the wheel-house. For, despite the flow of free drinks, the multi-purpose salon was deserted and darkened. The moon shone as brightly as before, but clouds were banking in the north east and already blanketed the gleam of the stars in that part of the sky. The air was still only given an illusion of movement by the forward thrust of the boat. But, if a norther was brewing, every light in the sky would be masked within minutes.

The half-breed's footfalls rang loud in his own ears against the decking as he moved along the companionway and out over the Boiler Deck towards the aft-sited toilets.

The signal lamp flashed three times from the Nebraska bank as he reached to open the door. Immediately, the engine note altered and the big paddle-wheel slowed. For a few moments, the impetus of the boat continued to push her through the water at the same speed, the drag of the slower turning-wheel making more white foam than usual. But then she slowed and her reduced way made her less responsive to the demands of her twin rudders against the powerful currents.

Edge remained where he was for a moment, peering at the

base of the bluff where the signal lantern had flashed.

The *Delta Dawn* shuddered and her bows inched around to starboard. Ice-floes crunched hard against her hull instead of her bow. White water showed against the pitch-black moon-shadow of sycamore timber growing under the bluff. Then a yawl was rowed out towards mid-river. Three men were mere silhouettes in the boat: two handling the oars while the third sat motionless on the stern gunwale. The tiny boat was still ahead of the dawdling stern-wheeler, the oarsmen rowing fast and expertly, on a semicircular course that was designed to turn the yawl upriver and close with the *Delta Dawn* amidships.

Edge stepped into the toilet, used it without haste, and came out. There was a burst of power from the engines, with the rudders hard over, to get the stern-wheeler on a due north heading again. Then she slowed, and something banged against her hull with more force than a small ice-floe.

The half-breed moved to the Boiler Deck rail, but stayed in the moonshadow of the toilet to lean out and look down at the main deck below. The yawl was alongside, just aft of the hold where Edge had slept through the afternoon. A bowline from the smaller craft was hitched around the rail and held fast by a man the half-breed failed to recognise. The mate, Wren, had a grip on the blade of an oar while the oarsman held the handle.

'Hurry it up, frig it!' Wren snarled through grimacing teeth. 'My arms are near broke!'

The man in the stern of the yawl was short, wiry and nimble. There was something of the lithe animal about him as he stood, reached for the rail, and hauled himself up and over on to the deck.

'When a fellow doesn't have either brains or skills, his only useful asset is brute strength,' the new passenger said arrogantly, his accent strongly British. 'Where?'

Wren released the oar and the bowline whipped free a moment later. Both oarsmen were on one side of the small boat and shoved hard against the hull of the *Delta Dawn*. Open water showed between the two craft and the men continued to fend off, using the full length of their oars. The yawl cleared the sucking action of the stern-wheel and then was rocked and pitched in the wake until the men had re-fitted the oars into the rowlocks and pulled hard for smooth water. Their safe escape was seen from the wheel-house and

51

full power was demanded from the engine again. Smoke belched faster and thicker from the twin stacks, the acrid black streams filled with bright, short-lived sparks.

Wren, the other man and the new passenger went from sight. As impassive as ever Edge started across the Boiler Deck: satisfied that he had seen the boarding but prepared to ignore it and its implications unless events made it his business.

The doors of the cabins were recessed about a foot into the bulkheads and the half-breed sensed the presence of another before he saw him. His coat had never been buttoned since he left Charity's cabin. As he became aware of a figure standing against the door of Ferris's private compartment, his right· hand was lifted slightly to curl the long, brown fingers against the coat – level with the Remington butt jutting from the tied-down holster.

'Easy, Captain,' Henry Rhett announced, stepping away from the door. 'On account of Bob, we're not enemies any more.'

He was grinning and Edge acknowledged the comment with a wry expression. Then: 'But we'll never get to be even just good friends, feller,' he said sourly.

Rhett's grin did not alter. 'Like I said, I can take a joke. No offence, Captain.'

'You sure won't commit one with me,' Edge rasped, and pushed open the door to enter Charity's cabin.

The woman was in a deep sleep, breathing regularly with just the suggestion of a low snore at the start of each inhalation. But the sounds of her sleeping were not loud enough to mask a short series of noises outside on the companionway: which began and ended just as Edge was about to close the door fully. The harsher, more insistent thud, splash and beat of the *Delta Dawn*'s progress might have covered the thump, groan and grunt – had not Edge turned to pull open the door and step outside again.

He recognised the sounds for what they were: the thump of something hard and heavy against flesh, the groan of one man sinking into unconsciousness and the grunt of another under strain.

Edge completed the turn, drew the Remington and eased the door open. Charity had not responded to the first draught of cold air. She did so now, with a moan in her sleep and a movement that drew her body into a warm ball under the blankets. She did not wake up. Edge turned sideways-on to the open doorway and swung his long leg wide to step out on to the companionway. His gun was held low, at the full reach of his arm, the muzzle aimed at the deck.

The *Delta Dawn*'s new passenger was down on his haunches, both hands under Rhett's armpits as he lowered the unconscious man to the deck. Rhett's head was sagged forward, chin on his chest and face hidden. But his attacker's head was high, face revealed to Edge in the bright, cold moonlight. It was the face of a man about forty, with sharp eyes, slightly crooked nose and mouthline twisted by a snarl.

Edge shifted his glinting eyes from the expression, to the man's right hand and back again. The man was holding a gun – but by the barrel in the same grip as when he had crashed the base of the butt against Rhett's skull. His victim's derby had fallen off, its crown badly dented. Rhett's hair was much darker in one place than elsewhere.

'I was told there was one,' the Englishman rasped, sharp eyes moving to look at his back-to-front gun, then flitting towards the half-breed again.

'Yeah, he's one, feller,' Edge replied, moving his Remington slowly up to aim it at the face as the expression softened slightly from the snarl to craftiness. 'But that ain't the way he likes to sleep with another, I figure.'

The sharp eyes were confused for a moment. 'What is your angle, sir?'

'Obtuse right now. But I aim to change it. You want to get up, feller? Best you leave the gun down there with Rhett.'

'What then? You'll kill me, no doubt.'

'Doubt makes a man careful.'

The Englishman did as he was told: first releasing the Navy Colt so that it clattered to the deck. Then he withdrew his hands from under Rhett's armpits and drew himself erect. The back of Rhett's head thudded against his boots. They were expensive boots, in keeping with his long coat buttoned high to the neck and his low-crowned, wide-brimmed hat. His eyes darted one way and then the other, and did not express disappointment when he saw there was no way to escape.

'I'll double whatever Ferris is paying you,' he said, and seemed excited by the idea. 'Name it.'

'Nothing, feller.'

'What?'

'Double nothing, it comes out at nothing.'

A sneer altered the Englishman's mouthline. His voice matched the look. 'Another stupid patriot.' He shuffled backwards a few inches, to remove his feet from under Rhett's head. 'Like him, I suppose?'

' 'No way like him, feller. Knock on the door.'

'You'll shoot me in cold blood if I don't?'

'Sure will be cold when it runs out of the bullet hole.'

'A gunshot would wake up the entire boat.'

'Obliged for your concern on my account, feller. Won't be your worry.'

The Englishman sighed, gave a short shrug, and turned towards the cabin door. 'I would ask to be accorded the rights and privileges of a prisoner of war,' he said with a sidelong glance towards Edge. 'I am no longer armed and I have surrendered.'

He raised a clenched fist and rapped his knuckles on the wooden panel. It was obvious that Horace Ferris had been pressed to the inside of the door, listening to the exchange. For, as the knock sounded, the door was wrenched wide.

Edge heard the Englishman's sharp intake of breath and saw his profile suddenly gripped by a look of horror.

'No!' the terrified man gasped, and took a backward step.

Moonlight glinted on spinning metal between the dark doorway and the back-stepping man. The man swung up his hands, but by then the knife had penetrated his clothing and found flesh. Skin and its underlay of tissue was opened up and the Englishman's gaping mouth suddenly snapped closed as the honed point of the blade cut into his heart.

Already dead, but with his nervous system still reacting, he banged against the companionway rail, teetered for a moment, then slammed down on to the deck. He became inert on his back, head rolled to the side so that his staring but glazed eyes peered sightlessly into an upside-down image of Rhett's face.

As if shocked into consciousness by the proximity of a fresh corpse, Rhett flicked open his own eyes.

'Holy Mother!' the roused man shrieked softly, whipping up into a sitting posture. 'Who the hell – '

'One of the enemy,' Horace Ferris said as he stepped on to the threshold of his cabin, his stout form clad in a white nightshirt. 'His name is Manx.'

Edge had already taken two long strides to cover the distance between the cabin doors. As Ferris turned towards him, his ruddy-complexioned face set in an expression of sadness, the half-breed swung his free hand. It bunched into a tight fist after it started to move, and the flatness between the

54

knuckle joints slammed viciously into the Southerner's nose. Ferris was unconscious on his feet, and toppled without a sound until his unsupported weight crashed to the cabin floor. Blood from his crushed nose was warm for an instant on Edge's fist, before the biting river air chilled it.

Rhett seemed unaware of the punch and its consequences. Still disorientated from his own period of unconsciousness, he tried to get to his feet, his eyes trapped by the dead man's stare. He fell hard to the deck again.

'Sonofabitch, help me get away from this damn corpse!' he pleaded.

Edge holstered the Remington and reached down one hand to fasten a grip over Rhett's shoulder. He pulled him erect with smooth and easy strength.

'What's happening?' Charity Meagher asked from the threshold of her cabin.

Edge released the trembling Rhett and glanced towards the woman. She was holding her topcoat together in front of her nakedness.

Rhett backed away from the corpse to stoop and retrieve his dented derby.

'Manx!' Charity gasped, and dragged up her fear-filled gaze to look from Edge to Rhett and back again. 'Is he dead?'

'If his heart's in the right place,' Edge muttered.

Rhett shook his head violently. 'I'm okay now.' He touched gingerly at the place where his hair was matted with crusted blood. 'Guess it was getting hit like that. But waking up to find those eyes staring at me like that, I . . . '

'Forget that!' Charity snapped. 'And get Manx inside out of sight.'

'Yeah,' Edge growled. 'A cat can look at a queen.'

CHAPTER FIVE

'He's killed Mr Ferris!' the woman gasped as she tripped and almost stumbled over the bulky heap of the unconscious man in the cabin.

The splashes of blood from the man's crushed nose looked very dark on the whiteness of his nightshirt. As Charity recoiled from the sight, Edge brushed past her and crossed the cabin to a shelf beside the bed.

'He'll live,' the half-breed growled as he struck a match and lit the bedside lamp, turning the wick high to allow light to flood in to every corner of the cabin. 'But maybe only long enough to answer some questions.'

'What do you mean?' the woman demanded huskily as Rhett dragged the corpse of Manx over the threshold.

'Depends,' Edge answered as he recrossed the cabin, stooped and lifted the inert Ferris out of the path of the corpse.

'Depends?' Charity croaked, her wide eyes hinting that she was not far from the brink of hysteria.

'On his answers.'

Edge dropped the unconscious man unceremoniously on to the rumpled bed. Then he jerked a blanket roughly out from under Ferris and tossed it towards Rhett. 'Cover him up and then stay by the door, feller. We could get company. Looking for trouble or maybe just checking for it.'

Rhett released his hold on the corpse in the middle of the cabin and used the blanket for a shroud. He went to stand by the door, but through the pain on his face was visible another emotion. His right hand was inside his jacket, resting close to the hole drilled through his clothing by the shot earlier.

'I heard your warning this morning, Captain,' he said evenly. 'But you can forget about me forgiving you after shooting Jase. For I'll sure do more than just point a gun at you if you try to hurt Mr Ferris any more.'

'It's gone midnight, so I'll remember that, feller,' Edge told him, glancing around the cabin and then dropping down on to his haunches.

'What's midnight got to do with it?' Rhett asked.

'Maybe you don't deserve two bad days in a row. So you could get lucky – if you've got the speed.'

He had been searching for something containing water: and failed to locate anything until he saw the chamberpot – which had been used.

Charity grimaced as he came erect, holding the pot with its acrid-smelling contents. 'I can explain!' she blurted out.

'You're quite an organ grinder, ma'am,' the half-breed growled. 'But it's this monkey I want to listen to right now. Need him awake for that.'

He tipped the pot and yellow urine splashed down over the blood-run face of Horace Ferris. The liquid, long cold from being out of his body, roused him to groaning awareness. Then its acid content burned the split skin inside his nostrils and he gritted his teeth as he snapped open his eyes. Their darkness was dull for a moment, then filled with the light of memory.

'You hit me!' he accused, keeping his head pressed hard against the pillow, while his eyes swivelled in their sockets: seeking to see the other people who he sensed were in the cabin.

'On account you killed an unarmed man while I was covering him with a gun, feller,' the half-breed responded, slowly, distinctly and with a total lack of emotion. 'That ain't my way. You got a good reason why I should overlook it this time?'

Ferris pushed out his tongue to lick his lips: then withdrew it quickly when he tasted the bitterness dripping out of his moustache. 'What did you wake me with?' he asked, and gagged on rising bile to show that he already knew the answer.

'When I'm pissed off, other people sometimes get to feeling the same way, feller.' Edge said evenly.

Ferris used the tips of both stubby index fingers to explore his damaged nose. 'I hurt bad.'

'Nobody ever hurts good. Possible to hurt a lot worse, though.'

'He's a dead man if he tries anything like that, Mr Ferris,' Rhett assured. 'Not everything Bob wrote about him was good.'

Ferris dropped his hands back to his sides. 'You knew Rhett's brother in the war, isn't that so?' His eyes, with grim

57

determination behind the pain, directed their stare towards the overhead bulkhead. 'Fighting on the side of the Federal forces?'

'He tell you how many times I spat while we took Lookout Mountain?' Edge asked sourly.

Because he did not try, Edge could not recall if Bob Rhett had been in his troop at Lookout and Missionary Ridge. When the name Rhett had been added to Henry earlier, the half-breed's mind had been flooded with countless memories. Predominant was a mental image of Bob Rhett's body sprawled beside that of Jamie in the yard of the ruined Iowa farm – the intestines of the New Englander swinging aloft in the hot air, from the beak of a triumphant buzzard.

Another strong image was of Trooper Rhett after the escape from a Richmond prison. Aboard a commandeered Confederate ironclad on the blood run down the James River. When the younger Rhett had announced he had a brother who was a Mississippi riverboat gambler before the war.

'There are some on the defeated side who would wish to restart the war, Captain,' Ferris said.

'I surrendered the rank when I gave up the uniform, feller.'

'He prefers to be called Edge, Mr Ferris,' Charity supplied.

The injured man seemed relieved to hear the woman's voice. His gaze shifted from the blank overhead to find the impassive face of Edge. 'Did you also surrender the hopes and values for which you fought the war?'

'No, feller. Lost them after it was all over.' There was a harshness in his tone.

'Edge likes to get straight to the point, Mr Ferris,' Charity prompted, with a trace of bitterness.

'Thank you,' Ferris told her, then to Edge: 'May I get up?'

The half-breed had delved into a shirt pocket to bring out the makings. He was wetting the paper to complete the cigarette. 'If you want to get knocked down again, feller.' He struck a match on the bulkhead.

Rhett shuffled his feet and cleared his throat as Edge hung the cigarette at the corner of his mouth. The half-breed whirled and drew the Remington in a single, smooth action. Rhett stared at the rock-steady gun in the tall man's fist and froze, his own hand still deep inside his coat.

'Something on your mind that means I don't have to kill you, big brother Rhett?' Edge asked.

The man at the door paled visibly, but Charity made a

throaty sound of disgust before he could speak.

'This is ridiculous!' she snapped, and moved forward, stepping across the line of fire. 'And I'm not scared of you, Edge.'

She crouched in front of a bureau, opened the lower doors and took out a basin and pitcher. There was water in the pitcher and she poured it into the basin. The splashing sound was very loud in the silence of the room.

Edge pushed the Remington back into the holster and Rhett withdrew his hand from inside his coat – empty. The grin he pasted on to his thin face did not entirely cancel out his earlier fear.

'You acted like you were on our side out there, Captain.'

Charity circled the bed to the other side from Edge. Ferris looked at her gratefully as she ripped a portion of sheet, soaked it in the icy water and began to wipe the blood and urine from his face.

'Acted for my own benefit, feller,' Edge corrected, and returned his attention to the grimacing Ferris and the defiant woman. 'Figured to hear both sides of the story.'

Charity had only partially cleaned up Ferris, but he pushed her hands away. 'Thank you, my dear.' His eyes, filled with earnestness, were directed up at the half-breed. 'Mr Edge, are you prepared to assist in preventing a reoccurence of secession and its bloody consequences?'

'One war is enough in anyone's lifetime, feller.'

'Meaning?'

'Trust him, Mr Ferris,' Charity urged. 'There are a lot of things he isn't, but I think he possesses a sense of honour.'

'Yes!' Ferris responded emphatically, and pulled himself up into a sitting position against the head of the bed. Edge continued to eye him coldly through the smoke rising from his cigarette. 'He proved that. I apologise, Mr Edge. For my over-reaction to seeing Edward Manx. But the mission with which I have been entrusted makes it essential that I act first and ask questions later.'

Edge dropped the cigarette, crushed it under his boot and jerked a thumb towards the draped corpse. 'He ain't saying much. Nor are you.'

Ferris nodded and sucked in a deep breath. 'Miss Meagher and I are agents of the United States Government, Mr Edge. We have been operating in New Orleans to uncover a plot that, if it succeeds, will plunge this country into another civil war.

59

'Miss Meagher and I were not working alone. There was a group of us and one of the group came into possession of a letter. A most damaging letter – for either patriots or traitors, depending upon who sees it.'

Edge thrust out a hand. 'You want to let me read it, feller?'

'I trust no man that much, sir!' Ferris snapped, then brought his voice under control. 'But I will tell you that it pledges money and allegiance to a new uprising of the southern states against the national government of this country. And that it is signed by sixty-seven of the most powerful, influential and wealthy citizens of this country. Men in government, business, commerce and industry. Each of whose position would, in the event of civil strife, be worth a thousand men in the Rebel army – in terms of the damage they could do to the defence of the nation.'

Ferris paused and both he and Charity waited anxiously for a response to the verbal bombshell.

'You must realise the vital importance of such a document, sir?' Ferris growled when the half-breed remained impassively silent.

Charity sighed. 'Edge is not the demonstrative type, Mr Ferris.'

'Unless his feelings are strong enough,' the injured man muttered, using his fingers to explore his damaged nose again.

The woman touched the bruise on her cheek raised by the half-breed's back-handed slap.

'Bob used to say he was a real cold fish most of the time,' Rhett supplied. 'Hell on two legs when the time was right, though.'

'Anyone got the right time?' Edge asked evenly.

'I intend to deliver the document into the hands of President Calvin Coolidge,' Ferris said hurriedly. 'The eight other members of our New Orleans group died in obtaining the letter. We all knew the dangers and we all knew that – because so many highly placed men in government had signed it – it was imperative that the president should receive it personally.

'Apart from obtaining the document, we have been fortunate in only one respect. Mr Coolidge is away from Washington at the moment – far removed from the men who appended their signatures to the letter and perhaps countless others of similar sympathies. He is at present on a hunting trip in the Dakotas, using Fort Sully as his base. It is there that Miss Meagher and I intend to hand him the letter.'

'Which he is unaware he is to receive,' Charity added. 'There are so many traitors in high places that we did not dare send word ahead about what we have.' Her tone became abruptly more solemn. 'Not all the group were murdered in obtaining the letter, Edge. One died because he attempted to communicate through normal channels and was betrayed to the enemy.'

'The channel this tub is following ain't exactly free of snags,' Edge pointed out flatly.

'We reached Omaha without incident,' Ferris said. 'But we have always known there was a strong possibility the Rebels would locate us. When Mr Rhett and his friends burst into the shipping company office, we thought it had happened then. We knew it was so when the attempt was made to assassinate me at the card table earlier this evening.'

'It was a set-up, Captain,' Rhett put in. 'Hold-ups and picking pockets aren't my style.'

'It showed, feller.'

Rhett ignored the remark. 'I'm a gambling man, but Lady Luck turned her back on me at the Omaha tables.'

'*She* had nothing to worry about.'

Again Edge's interruption was brushed aside, this time with a wave of the hand. 'I know cards, Captain. And I know all the tricks a man can work with cards. That guy tonight was working those pasteboards every way there is. Smooth and smart. But there was a switch from the normal routine. He was cheating to lose, and he dropped a bundle. Same as me and the kid with the rat face. And it was being done to make Mr Ferris win and look like it was he who was the crook.'

Rhett's grin of pride had a childlike quality about it.

'You were on the team when you used that crazy little gun?' Edge asked.

'It's French,' Rhett answered eagerly, still grinning. 'Called an Apache Knuckleduster. Don't ask me why.'

'That ain't the why I'm asking about, feller.'

The weakly handsome features of Henry Rhett became set in a solemn expression. 'Mostly on account of I'm broke, Captain. You loused up the robbery and I only got a small stake from lifting leather. Mr Ferris won most of that before I realised what was happening. And I figured he could use a bodyguard, after that guy pulled a gun.'

'The man at the card table was not known to me, Mr Edge,' Ferris amplified. 'And neither was Rhett until Charity told me he was one of the hold-up men. After Rhett explained the

61

shooting to the satisfaction of the ship's master, he offered his services to me. And I accepted, after explaining my situation and its dangers.

'Knowledge of these dangers caused me to act without thought – out of fear, if you like – when I saw Manx outside the door. Manx was known to me. He killed several of the group in New Orleans. I acted instinctively and I sincerely apologise for involving you in such a ruthless killing. But he was, himself, a dedicated murderer for his own cause, totally without scruples.'

'It's the truth, Edge,' Charity added. 'Everything we have told you is the absolute truth. If you believe us and are willing to help, you will not find Mr Ferris lacking in generosity. I was also telling the truth when I said he is a wealthy New Orleans businessman.'

'When he's not putting his life on the line for Uncle Sam?'

Ferris snorted. 'I can assure you I am not involved in this for glory, Mr Edge. I would be only too happy were my light hidden under a bushel. I am doing it because I feel I must. But I realise that, like Rhett, you require financial reward. I have advanced him five hundred dollars against a final payment of five thousand when I hand the letter to the President.'

'With no reduction for services already rendered by the school-teacher here?' the half-breed asked sourly.

Despite the circumstances, Charity was still able to flush with embarrassment.

'There is no need for shame, my dear,' Ferris assured her, then looked sheepishly at Edge. 'Our methods were crude in more than one sense,' he admitted. 'Again, my fear – for myself, Miss Meagher and our mission – is to blame. Despite the fact that the gunmen in Omaha were not sent by our enemies, we knew it was only a matter of time before they did find us. And your actions during the robbery attempt showed us you were just the kind of man we needed. But we could not be sure you shared our brand of patriotism, Mr Edge. Miss Meagher set her cap at you, as it were, to try to discover where your loyalties lay. In the last resort it proved an unnecessary ploy, for Rhett was able to tell me of your war record.'

'Not unnecessary, Mr Ferris,' Charity corrected. 'Edge was in the right place at the right time when a second attempt was made on your life. And I feel no shame for what I did.'

'You sure didn't while you were doing it, ma'am,' Edge

muttered, as he turned and reached the door in three strides.

'You will not help your country, sir?' Ferris called tightly.

'I already did, once,' Edge answered as Rhett stepped out of his path. 'It won and I lost. I ain't about to go back for more after that happened.'

'Can we at least rely upon your neutrality?' Ferris asked. 'Now that the Rebels know I'm aboard the *Delta Dawn*, there will be more attempts on my life.'

'Ain't nobody's business mine unless they make it so, feller.' As he reached for the door handle, he smiled wryly at Charity across a hand rasping his jaw bristles. 'Sure was a pleasure doing business with you, ma'am. Anything else is just bound to be an anticlimax.'

'Go to hell, Edge!' she snapped.

'Sorry you won't join us, Captain,' Rhett said as Edge opened the door. 'But I guess we can get along without you. That stuff with Manx isn't like me at all. Like Bob in the war, I can hold my own.'

'Yeah, he could hold his own all right,' the half-breed allowed with a wry curling back of his thin lips. 'But he liked it better when another feller held it for him.'

CHAPTER SIX

The cloud bank in the north east had tumbled to spread a
thick blanket of low, dark nimbostratus across the entire sky.
Every star was masked and there was not even a faint glow to
mark the position of the moon. The decking was slippery under
Edge's boots as he went forward to the stairway. From time
to time, the bow of the stern-wheeler rose and the whole boat
juddered as she cracked the larger ice-floes. She was making
only half speed through the dark night, veering from one side
of the river to the other to avoid hitting the largest floes and
the dangerous snags of uprooted tree-trunks which either
floated free on the currents or were imbedded in the mud.

The twin stacks smoked and the paired engines rumbled. The
big stern-wheel turned.

Edge moved down the stairway from the Hurricane Deck
and started aft, the biting chill of the early hours' air causing
him no regret that he had relinquished the opportunity to share
Charity Meagher's bed. For his mind was concerned with the
pros and cons of the offer Ferris had made him. Pondering the
question of whether he had been right or wrong to turn down
five thousand dollars simply because Ferris and the woman had
injured his pride. Deciding that, in truth, he had allowed
himself to be suckered: had chosen to ignore the facts of adja-
cent cabins and not so secret exchanges of looks that linked
Ferris and Charity Meagher together. Had ignored the signs,
and therefore allowed his guard to drop, for the simple reason
that he felt the need of a woman.

The conclusion angered him, for experience had taught him
time and time again that his ruling destiny did not allow him
the luxury of human relationships that were more than wafer
thin. Or, if they were allowed, it was only so that fate could
take a cruel twist and cause him more suffering.

He was on the companionway of the main deck now. Something limp and heavy dropped through the cold air on the

periphery of his vision. He turned his head fast, in time to see the doubled-up corpse of the Englishman splash into the icy river. The once human piece of detritus was immediately sucked down under the surface, to be sent southwards and tossed up to float far behind the *Delta Dawn*.

Edge grinned, his period of self-anger finished. It had been good with the woman and perhaps, had she been simply what she claimed, he might still have been enjoying her. But circumstances made this purely academic. She had used him and he, in turn, had used her. On his part, lust and its release had no depth. He felt nothing for her, so in losing her he had lost nothing which could not be replaced should the need arise again. Except the comfort and warmth of her bed. And even at the best times in his life – when Josiah C. Hedges or Edge – comfort had never been high in his priorities.

He reached the hatchway, closed against the night, which gave on to the hold where his stinking bedding waited for him. He pushed it open and looked at a man standing just inside the threshold. It was the roustabout the Negro had called Irish. The man was holding a shotgun with its double barrels sawn off short. The base of the stock was braced against his bulbous belly, his left hand steadying the barrels and his right folded around the frame, a finger curled to both triggers.

'You can just disappear in mysterious circumstances, mister,' the roustabout said softly. 'Or we can tell McBride how we caught you stealin' from Mr Wren. We can do that while we're hosin' what's left of you off the deck, mister.'

'Just the two choices?' Edge asked, sensing that a man was approaching along the deck from the stern.

'And two men to make sure that's all there is, Edge.'

The other man was the mate, the Colt drawn from his belt and aimed at the half-breed.

There was a great deal of snoring and deep breathing in the darkness of the hold behind Irish.

'Make up your mind,' Wren insisted.

Edge eyed the twin muzzles of the shotgun ruefully. 'Figure this isn't the time to go to pieces,' he muttered and turned towards Wren.

The mate backed off two steps and thrust the Colt out in front of him, gripping it two handed, arms up level with his shoulders.

'Open your coat and let Irish take your gun.'

Edge did as he was told, his posture casual but beneath the

surface poised to power into movement should the opportunity arise. But the Colt did not waver in its aim and Irish confiscated the Remington with smooth speed. There was a splash as the gun was tossed over the side. Then the shotgun nudged the small of his back.

'Move aft, mister.' The hatch to the hold was quietly closed. 'If I have to blast your guts out, that'll be the place where Mr Wren and me caught up with you. You'll have Mr Wren's gold watch in your pocket. You understand, mister?'

'Yeah,' Edge replied, starting forward as Wren backed away from him. 'I don't even have to take the time.'

There were no obstructions on the deck until the aft port cleat was reached. Wren knew this and halted short, never having to look over his shoulder, and keeping his aim constant. When he stopped, Edge halted and the pressure of the shotgun muzzles was relieved from the base of his spine.

Beyond the bulkhead beside which they stood, the port engine rumbled, drawing steam power from the forward boilers and turning it into energy to rotate the stern-wheel. The wheel thrashed at the water and the overhead steam-escape pipe hissed.

'I do something to you fellers?' Edge asked, having to raise his voice to be heard above the frenetic noise.

He was ready to make his move now, fear of death and ambition to survive having brought his muscles to the peak of hair-trigger tension. He knew his initial target was going to be Irish, who could not fail to do him damage with the spreading double load of the shotgun. Should he get the chance to fire it.

'Joined the opposition, Edge!' Wren yelled, altering the aim of the Colt to draw a bead on the half-breed's chest. 'I was outside the cabin door when Ferris hired you.'

Edge leaned backwards from the waist: just a fraction of an inch. The twin muzzles nudged him again.

Wren smiled his confidence. 'Any consolation to you, Rhett, the dame and Ferris won't be long in feeding the fish. Same as you and Manx.'

'No consolation for me. Only interested in first prize.'

His arms were down at his sides, apparently limp in surrender to the inevitable.

Wren's finger became taut around the Colt trigger, the smile broadening on his heavily stubbled, deeply weathered face.

Irish's boots scraped on the decking and the shotgun was withdrawn from resting against the half-breed's back.

Edge whirled, his right arm swinging ahead of his body, stiff and away from his side. At the same time, he powered into a half crouch. And it was the back of his elbow that hit the shotgun.

Instinctively, Irish tightened his grip on the weapon: so that the force of Edge's arm impacting with the barrels sent the man into the start of a spin. Irish began an obscenity, which became a shriek of alarm.

Edge thought this was because the roustabout feared an impulsive shot from Wren's Colt could tear into his flesh.

But no gun exploded.

The half-breed had his back towards Wren, his right hand curving up to fasten on the twin barrels of the shotgun.

Irish fought him, going into a crouch of his own and then trying to lunge backwards and wrench the weapon from Edge's grasp.

Edge's left hand swung up to the nape of his neck, delved under the collar and his hair: then streaked into view again, fisted around the handle of the razor.

For an instant, he submitted to the strength of Irish, allowing the snarling roustabout to think he was on the verge of snatching the gun free.

But it was only a feint. When the roustabout yanked on the gun, Edge maintained his grip and went with the power of the pull. Then up on his toes to add to the momentum.

Arching his body to stay clear of the barrels, he lunged forward, and pulled on the gun again.

Irish was forced into a half turn and Edge seemed to glide around him, with the shotgun as a rotating lever and the roustabout as an axis.

Over the broad shoulder of Irish, Edge saw the reason for the man's earlier cry of alarm – and the reason why Wren had not blasted a bullet into his back.

For the mate was trapped in a vicious bearhug, applied from behind by the Negro named Linn. Wren still held the Colt in a double-handed grip and his finger continued to be curled around the trigger. But one of Linn's hands was also wrapped around the butt, forcing the barrel deep into the flesh beneath the mate's jaw. Stark terror was inscribed into the leathery skin.

'Some dance you're doin', man,' the Negro called. 'Got a name to it?'

The roustabout tried again to jerk the shotgun free and

67

swing it on to target. Edge swivelled sideways-on to the barrel, sucked in his belly and leapt towards the riverman. His left arm came up and slashed crossways. The point of the razor followed the contours of the man's upper face – digging fractionally below the surface. Into the sparse flesh at the right temple, through the membrane of the right eye, over the bridge of the nose and sliced the lid which closed by reflex over the left eye. The riverman was screaming then, the sound rising to a high pitch of shrillness when Edge applied more pressure to the razor: to sink it through the lid and deep into the eye.

He released his hold on the shotgun and Edge let go a split second later. As the weapon clattered to the deck, the roust-about threw his hands up to his face, a moment after the half-breed withdrew the wounding blade.

'My eyes!' he screamed, staggered to the rail, bounced off and spun in blind circles to bang into the bulkhead.

'Irish reel?' Edge suggested to the Negro.

Linn laughed, his white teeth gleaming in the faint light from the distant wheel-house.

'Help me?' the Irish roustabout pleaded, flinging his arms to the sides, then ahead of him. From his forehead to his jaw, his face was dark and slick with fresh blood.

The icy dampness of a new blizzard began to drop through the darkness.

Irish staggered to the rail. Edge went with him, ducked under the flailing arms and slashed the razor up between them. The blade sank into the base of the blinded man's throat and cut upwards until the jawbone forced a withdrawal. Irish started a new scream of agony, but it became a gurgle as blood flooded into his sliced-open windpipe. Crimson spittle sprayed from his gaping mouth.

'You the only man allowed to cut in?' Linn yelled gleefully.

Irish made to topple backwards, but Edge used his free hand to grasp the scruff of the dying man's neck. He bent him forward over the rail, then hooked a boot in front of Irish's ankles and raised the spasming legs. Irish died, bent double over the rail. Edge tipped him into the river.

'Guess he only had eyes for me,' the half-breed growled, and stooped to pick up the discarded shotgun. It was a once ornate and now well-used centre-fire Daw's which broke open for loading. He eased the hammers back to the rest. 'I owe you, feller? Or you have a personal interest?'

Wren was unconscious, either from having his breathing stopped by the strength of Linn's grasp or because he had fainted from fear.

'Saw that Irish sonofabitch get the drop on you, man. Came out the hold on the starboard side to take a look see. When this bastard showed, I evened up the odds. No real favour man. I owe him. Nothin' good.'

'Be obliged if he could live awhile longer,' the half-breed said with a nod.

Linn opened his arms and Wren slid to the deck. The boarding was crusted with a layer of frozen snow. But the fall had been short. The cloud cover stayed low and solid but the wind held off. Wren's unfeeling hands continued to grip the Colt until Linn plucked the gun from between the stiff fingers.

'You want me to back off while you do your business with him, man?' the Negro asked, his excitement gone: replaced by resolute patience. 'Just like to be in at the death, if that's all right?'

Edge crouched down beside the inert Wren and wiped the razor clean of blood on the mate's uniform coat. 'Anything you like about the South?' he asked. 'Back in the early sixties?'

Linn gathered saliva into his mouth and spat it at the bulkhead. It instantly froze. 'Was pickin' cotton in South Carolina early on. Got outta that fast and joined the Union's 107th Coloured Infantry. I ain't never been south of the old Mason-Dixon since, man.' He directed his gaze and his newly acquired Colt along the deck towards the bow. 'Company. The feminine kind.'

Edge looked over his shoulder and saw the familiar silhouette of Charity Meagher. The woman was advancing tentatively across the Main Deck, the bulkiness of her clothing showing she now wore more than just the top coat.

'Edge?' she called, shrill and nervous.

'In one, ma'am,' he answered.

She quickened her pace, almost slipping over on the icy boarding. Then halted short, moving fast glances between the towering Linn and the unconscious Wren.

The Negro showed a shy smile and pushed the Colt into his belt.

'He's on your side,' Edge growled, pointing. His hand moved to indicate the mate. 'He ain't.'

Charity swallowed hard, unsure of her emotions and the expression she should wear on her pretty face. 'I came to find

69

you,' she blurted out. 'To explain about . . . how it was . . . that it wasn't – '

Wren groaned, in response to a new judder of the boat as she hit another ice-floe.

'Another time and a better place, Charity,' the half-breed interrupted, and his use of her name again inspired surprise, then something close to a smile.

'What happened?'

Wren groaned again and his eyelids flickered.

'He and another feller made your business my business. The other feller's all through with regret about it.'

He used the razor to scrape up some frozen snow, pulled Wren's jaw down and dropped the ice into the mouth. The mate choked back to full awareness.

'Him?' Charity asked, with an anxious glance at Linn.

'No. His black looks are all for the other side,' Edge answered, and shifted his narrow-eyed gaze towards the Negro. 'You can stick around.' Then, to Wren as the mate's expression altered from confusion to terror: 'They got anybody better than you lined up, feller?'

A few more flakes of snow fell. They clung to the clothing, faces and hair of the quartet grouped beside the engine-room bulkhead.

'I don't know nothin',' Wren rasped.

Edge rested the shotgun on the deck, clamped his left hand over Wren's mouth and moved the razor. His action and his expression were as chillingly cold as the dark night. Wren's outward gust of breath was burning hot against his palm – the scream which it powered like a distant bird cry. The mate's left ear lay on the frozen snow, blood from it and the side of his head looking black and ugly against the whiteness.

Charity gasped and backed away.

Linn vented a short laugh.

The woman slipped and crashed hard to her rump.

Edge leaned close to Wren's remaining ear as the woman struggled to her feet and retreated more carefully. 'Don't have a lot of time for fellers who try to kill me. Take you long to convince me it's the truth?'

He lifted his hand from the man's mouth and Wren moaned, his eyes swivelling far over to seek out the hacked-off portion of his flesh. He didn't like the view and stared up into the face of Edge. The snowflakes clinging to the dark stubble of the half-breed gave the lean features with the glinting eyes and curled-back lips a look of almost demonic evil.

'They won't give up,' he rasped. 'I didn't know about the poker game. Only about Manx comin' aboard. When that didn't work, Irish and me decided to make things easier. That's the truth. Gospel honest.'

'The Lord don't mean nothin' to you, white trash!' Linn snarled.

Wren's eyes moved again, while his head stayed immobile. He saw the Negro and was gripped by an even greater terror: becoming aware for the first time that it was Linn who had bearhugged him.

'I swear it, Edge!' the mate pleaded. 'They'll keep tryin' until they do it! But it ain't gotta look like it really is. They don't want the stuff to start flyin' yet. I can't tell you no more.'

'Obliged,' Edge said, wiping the razor on Wren's coat again before he slid it back into the neck pouch. Then he picked up the shotgun and straightened. 'All through.' he told Linn.

Wren was no longer feeling pain. For the bitter cold had numbed the blood-caked wound at the side of his head. Then a new wave of terror froze him into total paralysis as the Negro advanced to assume the half-breed's previous position – squatting down beside him. He could only work his lower lip, and even then no sound came out.

'You gave me hell, white trash,' Linn said dispassionately, just loud enough for his voice to carry above the noise of the *Delta Dawn*'s progress to where Edge stood against the rail. 'Worked me harder than any other man on this firetrap. Give me all the shit jobs and got me in bad with McBride every chance you got. Just because I'm black. Worse of all, never called me anything but nigger. You remember all that, white trash?'

Wren had his lips compressed now, and was breathing fast through his flaring and contracting nostrils.

Edge sensed the eyes of the woman on him and knew they were imploring him to do something. Even though his back was towards her when he sliced off Wren's ear, he had felt the hatred and revulsion she was staring at him. But he had thought it was a passing phase: that she detested the streak of cruelty in him but would overlook it when the circumstances of the moment were passed. Her motives for overlooking it did not concern him. He ignored her now, as he rolled a cigarette, the shotgun pressed to the side of his body by one arm.

71

Linn moved his position, down towards Wren's feet. The mate was as still as a waking corpse, trapped in a coma of terror.

'Ain't gonna soil my hands or my blades on your flesh, white trash,' the Negro said, almost crooning. 'But I sure am gonna kill you, mister friggin' mate.'

Snowflakes floated down, then stopped. The boat juddered against a snag that was not floating free, but came clear with a hard turn to starboard. Linn crouched at Wren's feet, grasped a boot in each hand and stood up. With the ease of great strength, he lifted the mate, and raised his arms above his head so that Wren was hanging upside down, just the backs of his hands brushing the deck.

Linn carried his unstruggling burden along the deck, to a gap in the rail where a gangplank was positioned when the stern-wheeler was docked.

Edge ambled after him as Charity Meagher backed away.

'It's all them times he called me nigger, missy,' Linn explained to the woman. 'That's why I hate him so much.'

He turned into the gap, to swing Wren out over the water slurping along the hull of the boat. He bent his legs at the knees and ankles. Wren's hands broke through the surface and he was abruptly exploded out of his paralysis. His scream was piercingly shrill. He tried to kick his feet free of Linn's hold. Linn crouched deeper and the scream was curtailed as the mouth from which it was vented closed against the rush of water.

The feet kicked once more, then were still. Linn continued to crouch and hold his burden as the corpse canted, the river seeking to snatch another unwanted piece of humanity. Stretched seconds passed, then the Negro straightened, hauling Wren out of the water. Drips fell from the head of the corpse, but not for long. Ice formed in the hair and on the face, giving Wren's upside-down features an even more grotesque appearance.

Linn grinned at Edge, the expression one of genuine humour. 'He don't ever do it again, man.'

'Give you a hard time?'

'Call a spade a spade!' His entire body quaked with laughter, and he released his grip on Wren's ankles.

The corpse splashed into the water and was immediately dragged down below the surface.

'That was ghastly!' Charity groaned as both Edge and the Negro leaned over the side to watch as the body bobbed to the surface astern of the boat, dark against the white water of the wake. 'I think I'm going to be sick to my stomach.'

'You changed your mind?' the half-breed asked, striking a match and touching it to the fresh-rolled cigarette. When he turned towards her, there was still a look of revulsion contorting her face. 'Something you said awhile back,' he added as he took hold of her faintly trembling arm.

'You ain't joinin' us poor folk in the hold, man?' the Negro called after them, and laughed again. A lighter sound than before. 'But I got no hard feelin's about it.'

'You wouldn't get it if you did have,' Edge answered him wryly, quickening his pace to hurry the woman back to her cabin.

'Changed my mind about what?' Charity asked at length, as they started up the stairway to the Hurricane deck.

Edge showed her a grin that was part coldly humorous and part mean. 'Liking chilled Wren.'

CHAPTER SEVEN

Henry Rhett was back on guard outside the door to Ferris's cabin. He stiffened and made to draw his hand out from inside his coat when Edge and Charity approached. Then recognised them and his grin held more than a trace of relief.

'You had second thoughts, Captain?' he asked. He put both hands to his mouth, cupped them and blew into them.

'There's been some trouble,' Charity said, shivering: from the cold and the memory. 'Edge has joined us.'

'Trouble?'

'Couple of fellers died,' the half-breed told him. 'No funeral expenses, but Ferris will be out another five thousand at the end of this trip. I'll relieve you in an hour.'

He stood aside to allow the woman to go in ahead of him. She had not yet recovered from seeing him torture a man and then stand idly by while Linn committed brutal murder. So, although she followed the tacit order and entered the cabin, her face wore a stiff mask of contempt.

'It sure will be good to have you – ' Rhett began.

'No way,' Edge cut in, and followed the woman, slamming the door on the outside cold and enjoying a moment of relative comfort before his flesh adjusted to a temperature that was just a few degrees higher.

'I wanted to tell you that it wasn't entirely a reluctant decision I came to, Mr Edge,' Charity said from close to the bed.

'This time you'll get longer to talk,' he replied, unfastening his coat. 'Afterwards.'

'I don't feel able to . . . ' She could not find a suitable way to end the sentence and let it hang in the chill air.

'Already told you rape ain't my way. Intend to share your bed, though. Up to you whether I do anything else but sleep in it.'

She was still fully dressed by the time he had stripped to his

74

underwear. As he advanced on the bed, she moved hurriedly away. He had his clothes bundled in his arms, the razor pouch and shotgun balanced on top. He moved a chair closer to the bed, dropped his burden into it and cocked both hammers of the gun. Then, totally ignoring her, he got under the covers, pressed his head into the pillow and covered himself to his chin.

'You'll hear me out!' she insisted, not moving closer. Her tone was of grim determination. 'It was entirely my idea to get you interested in me. Mr Ferris was strongly against it. But I could not have envisaged such a plan were the man not . . . not attractive to me. If I cheapened myself for something I believe in it was at least with a man I felt something for.

'But I no longer feel anything for you, Mr high and mighty Edge. When killing is inevitable in the pursuit of my cause, I accept it. But I do not relish it, and I can have no admiration for anybody who does so.'

She paused, and leaned forward to stare hard across the cabin at the bed, with its covers contouring the form of the half-breed.

'Are you listening to me?' she demanded.

Edge did not have the intention of sleeping. He had slept most of the afternoon and had felt anything but tired as he held Charity's arm when he escorted her to the cabin. Even though she had made her feelings blatantly plain on entering the cabin, he still felt a hard want for her: his mind recalling the first time for a long time.

But he was prepared to accept the warmth of her bed instead of the heat of her aroused body if that was the way it had to be. And the warmth beneath the covers had a quality of luxury after the biting cold of the pre-blizzard on deck. Then, despite the angry voice of the woman intruding upon the regular sounds of the *Delta Dawn*'s progress he began to feel drowsy. He heard nothing she said and was aware, in the moments before sleep wrapped his mind in comforting darkness, of a disturbing thought.

That perhaps he was getting old.

'Damnation!' Charity snarled, with the force of an obscene exclamation. Then controlled herself and shivered. Muttering to herself about male arrogance and her own determination not to be robbed of what was hers, she swept across the cabin, kicked off her shoes and eased into the bed otherwise fully dressed.

The sleeping half-breed was subconsciously aware of her proximity, but received no disturbing signals that she threatened danger. And he did not wake until the hour he had specified had elapsed. By that time, the warmth of the bed, augmented by the body heat of Edge, had worked to calm the woman to an extent where the need for sleep overtook her. Edge, aroused by a mental alarm, took no pains to be quiet as he dressed and armed himself, but Charity slept on peacefully.

Outside, snow and sleet were falling fast and every exposed surface of the *Delta Dawn* was coated with at least two inches of pure whiteness, sparkling with ice crystals. The Nebraska bank of the river, opposite the port side of the boat, was just visible through the falling flakes. The wind was coming in short gusts, veering constantly so that sometimes it blew from due north, sometimes east of north.

The open water between the stern-wheeler and the bank was narrowing. The big paddle-wheel alternately churned and stalled. Men's voices yelled, indistinct against the other sounds aboard.

'It seemed like frigging two hours, Captain,' Rhett growled, stamping his feet and blowing on his hands. His face was tinged with blue and the snow in front of Ferris's cabin door was hard packed.

'It wasn't,' the half-breed told him. 'Scheduled stop?'

'Yeah, to take on cordwood. And damn lucky there's safe mooring here. I reckon the pilot's been setting a course blind for the last mile. I'll see you, Captain.'

He turned to the door, then looked back to express a cold-pinched grin. 'I'm not getting any bonus like you are with the dame, Captain. Ferris and me don't sleep together.'

Edge nodded. 'Guess you're on the camp bed?'

'Shit!' Rhett growled. 'Bob used to write me you were real hard-nosed when a guy needed some fellow-feeling.'

'But he usually got some feller in the end,' Edge responded as the door closed on Rhett.

For a while, there was a continuance of activity aboard the *Delta Dawn* as she was steered towards the bank, then alongside a timber wharf: where man leapt ashore fore and aft to secure the mooring lines. Then the engines were disengaged and idled and the boilers were fired just enough to maintain a head of steam.

As if the weather felt it owed something to the snow-covered

76

stern-wheeler, the wind did nothing more than gust and veer until she was safely moored. Then it became a vengeance-ridden norther, howling directly down the line of the river and lashing at every obstacle with pelting snow, sleet and hail.

Roustabouts sent ashore to begin replenishing the boat's fuel reserves from ready-cut cordwood stacked on the wharf were hurriedly ordered back aboard. Soon, the howl of the wind, the crash of waves against the hull and wharf and the creak of the stern-wheeler's timber against pilings blanketed all other sounds. Surrounded by the blinding, lashing, swirling snowfall, Edge had a feeling of isolation. Beneath his feet the *Delta Dawn* rose and fell at the dictates of the storm-ravaged river: reminding him, if he needed an aid to memory, that he was aboard boat in close proximity to many fellow humans.

His eyes, narrowed to slits in concentration and defence against the wind and snow, constantly searched for the first sign of movement not caused by the blizzard. But the expression on his lean, heavily bristled face betrayed no hint of expectation – certainly not of fear that somebody might emerge from the storm with the intent of killing him.

Beneath the unrevealing surface of his near impassiveness, he was enjoying the sense of being apart from the rest of the world.

Even when he was no more than a boy, very much part of a close-knit family working the Iowa farmstead, he had been happiest doing those chores which required no help from others. During the war, his status as a junior officer allowed him little opportunity to carry out his duties alone and in his own way. And when his loner instincts did come into play, they aroused resentment among his men and drew the valid criticism that he was trying to win the war entirely on his own.

Since the war, he had been the true and ultimate loner on only two occasions – when he tracked down and killed Jamie's killers and then when he was only partially successful in finding those responsible for Beth's death.

Much as he had loved Beth, he had often during their tragically brief marriage, found himself compelled to go off alone into the rugged terrain of the Dakotas: for no other reason than to be his own man thinking his own thoughts, completely detached from the rest of humanity.

Before and since Beth there had been other brief periods

of self-inflicted solitude. Riding the high country, travelling the deserts and plains and even in countless hotel rooms of cities or towns. But always when there was no responsibility to anyone except himself: his single aim was to survive.

But a man could not survive by the gun alone. He had to eat, drink and have shelter from the elements. So he had to have money. In the case of the man called Edge, to earn money was essential for survival for despite everything else he had become he remained honest. He might kill a man who stole a dollar from him: but if there were ten thousand dollars on the corpse, Edge would take just one.

This need to earn money enforced human companionship on him and when a man placed himself in the service of another for reward, he was no longer his own man: he might try to convince himself he was working alone towards his own ends, but could never wholly accept the basic untruth.

Except for short intervals, such as now, standing alone in the freezing cold on the constantly moving deck of the stern-wheeler. Subconsciously, Edge knew he was guarding the life of Horace Ferris and that he had allies in Henry Rhett and Charity Meagher. Just as, beneath the sense of detachment from the world at large, he did not ignore the knowledge that there were many people close by. But the reality – against which he maintained vigilant guard – did not prevent him relishing his solitude in the blizzard.

Nature became calm as the new day was born. At first, the norther slackened, then veered and gusted with bursts of re-newed power. The snowfall thinned and broke up into squally showers. The Missouri continued to rush frenetically towards its distant meeting with the Mississippi, but its surface was less scarred by white water. The clouds slowed in their race south-wards and were thinned as they were sucked higher. Dawn injected greyness across the dark sky. The landscapes of Nebraska and Iowa became visible, their every feature thickly layered with pure white. The *Delta Dawn* rode high and taut against the wharf and her mooring lines.

Edge shook snow off his hat and brushed it from his shoulders. As the air became still it felt colder than at the height of the blizzard and he continued to pace a short course up and down the deck outside the cabin door. The shotgun remained trapped between his ribs and the inside of his right arm as he blew into his cupped hands.

He saw men on the shore before the roustabouts responded

78

to the bellowed order that aroused them from their bedrolls and sent them reluctantly towards the gangplanks.

The refuelling stop was at a point where the river cut through a stand of timber: the only feature of any significance for as far as the eye could see across the rolling prairie of Nebraska and Iowa. Once, the stand had been more extensive, but many of the trees had been felled to supply the Missouri steamboats with cordwood. The stumps of the sacrificed timber stood like giant, headless toadstools against the pure whiteness of the snow. The surviving trees, their boughs weighed down by snow, were huddled close together in two groups behind the wharf – split by a wagon track that ran due west from the river.

It was on this track that the men could be seen: about a dozen of them, bulky in warm clothing, urging their mounts through ice-crusted snow that touched the bellies of the smaller horses. The riders were still more than a quarter of a mile away when Edge first saw them.

As the roustabouts swarmed on to the wharf, carrying shovels with which they began to clear a path to a stack of cordwood, the door of a small shack swung open and another man appeared.

'Sure was a bad one!' he yelled, rubbing sleep from his eyes and squinting against the brightness of first light on snow.

'Held us up, damn it!' McBride shouted from the wheelhouse. 'And lost us two men.'

Smoke was whisping from the chimney of the wood-cutter's hut. The man looked longingly back inside his home before he closed the door on the warmth and trudged through the snow. He was middle-aged, short and thin under his thick, ankle-length coat. A heavy beard sprouted from his chin. His small eyes were red rimmed, from lack of sleep or a hangover.

'Lost 'em?'

'Overboard before we tied up, I reckon,' McBride answered sourly. 'Wren and a roustabout. Sure didn't jump ship in this God-forgotten white hell, Fryer.'

'I like it!' Fryer bellowed, and vented a trickle of shrill laughter. Then his tone became one of complaint as he looked from the boat to the men on the trail and back again. ' 'Ceptin' when folks come around clutterin' up the place.'

It was apparent the wood-cutter was a little unhinged: perhaps made that way by the loneliness of his occupation. Maybe, Edge thought briefly, he was himself a little deranged

79

because he enjoyed his own company so much.

There were eight roustabouts on the dock, their snow shovelling chore over now. Fryer, full of his own importance, was superintending the taking of logs from the stock to the boat. The blizzard was now completely blown out and the loudest sound was of steam hissing from escape valves.

The horsemen rode their mounts on to the dock and slid from their saddles, not talking. But one man emerged as the leader. He had ridden slightly ahead of the group and the others watched him closely, following his actions in reining his horse and dismounting.

The door behind Edge opened and Rhett emerged from the cabin. He smelled, for a moment, of sleeping in his clothes. Then the biting air of the lightening dawn neutralised the rancid odour. He fisted grit from his eyes and massaged the bristles of his face with both hands.

He surveyed the dismounted riders with a jaundiced gaze. 'I don't like the look of those guys, Captain.'

'You got your mind on the job?' Edge asked.

'Damn right. There's a time and a place for everything.'

The half-breed moved to the rail and Rhett joined him. The men continued to stand in a tight group with their horses, a few yards away from the wood stock, not talking as they watched the loading process. Their faces were blue and pinched by the cold: impassive beneath hatbrims and between the upturned collars of their coats.

'Good time and place for a raid,' Edge answered, after glancing up and down the river to find it still deserted.

'Boat I was aboard on the Mississippi got hit by raiders one time, Captain. But the guys got on at different stops. Didn't join up until they were ready to – '

The leader of the group had unbuttoned his coat. He looked to be in the same late-twenties age group as the rest. Under the coat he was dressed Western style, complete with gunbelt and tied-down holster. The gun he drew was an Army Colt. It came out of the holster slowly and the man looked at it with an air of distaste.

'Captain!' Rhett rasped.

'Tell Ferris it's time for trust, feller,' Edge answered softly, turning his back to the rail and unbuttoning his own coat. 'He gives the letter to you and you give it to the woman.'

It was uncomfortable, having the shotgun stuck into the

80

front of his gunbelt. But the coat was loose fitting enough to fasten again.

'What's she to do with it, Captain?'

'Use her imagination.'

As Edge turned around again, a man shouted: and a shot rang out.

'What if he won't give it me?'

'Kill him or count me out.'

It had been Fryer who yelled, as the leader of the group swung towards him: and aimed the Colt at him across ten feet of undisturbed snow. The bullet drilled a neat hole through the front of Fryer's coat and the thin wood-cutter flipped over backwards. A final pump of the dying heart spurted bright crimson across the pure whiteness of the snow. Fryer collasped like one of his felled trees. The roustabouts were immediately as still as the corpse, sculptured into attitudes of lifting logs and carrying them towards the gangplanks. For a stretched second it seemed that the only movement in the entire world was of the men behind the killer sliding Winchester rifles from their saddle-boots. And the only sounds, the working of the lever actions against the hiss of escaping steam.

Some of the rifles were aimed at the roustabouts and others at the wheel-house above the deck where Edge stood. Rhett was no longer at his side, having backed away and entered the cabin of Horace Ferris.

'What the – ?' Ferris asked.

'Got a proposition, Mr Ferris,' Rhett started, then closed the door on the rest of it.

'He's to show we mean business, sailor boy!' the killer called, loud, but in a lazy, conversational tone. 'Kill every sailor boy down here and a lot of folk aboard you don't do like you're told.'

He was looking up at the wheel-house.

A door opened behind Edge to the left.

'What's happening?' Charity asked fearfully.

'Stay inside!' Edge rasped through clenched teeth, his lips hardly moving. 'Expect a visitor.'

'Who are those men?'

'We haven't been introduced, lady. Just shut your mouth, then the door.'

Elsewhere, on the upper and lower decks, doors and hatches were flung open in response to the single shot.

The leader of the group had holstered his Colt. From one pocket of his coat he drew three sticks of dynamite, lashed together with tape. From another, his hand emerged holding a match. He struck it on a thumb-nail. There were screams and gasps as the match flared brightly. In the still air it burned without flickering.

'Shuddup!' the man snarled, loud and viciously angry. The command brought silence and he allowed the match to fall. It did not go out until it touched the snow. He drew out another match, but did not strike it. 'Folks'll die and your boat'll be so much driftwood on the Missouri, McBride. If that's what you want.'

'What do you want?' the master of the *Delta Dawn* demanded, his voice taut with fear.

'These guys to move into a nice, tight group,' came the response, with a wave of the dynamite to encompass the roustabouts. 'So we can cover them easy.'

He paused, a quizzical look on his heavy stubbled face.

'Do it!' McBride yelled.

'Quick or dead,' the leader of the group augmented.

The roustabouts complied, hurrying to crowd together at a spot indicated by the man with the dynamite. Some dropped their burden of logs and others did not. The door of Ferris's cabin opened.

'He said you'd better be straight, Captain,' Rhett growled, heading for the door of the neighbouring cabin.

'Figured it wasn't you who said it,' Edge muttered, moving towards the Hurricane Deck as Rhett entered the woman's cabin without knocking.

The man with the dynamite shared one ability with the half-breed: he could appear nonchalant and at ease while maintaining a careful surveillance of his surroundings.

'Everyone aboard stay still!' he snarled, and his dark eyes stared viciously at Edge for a moment. Then began to rake the boat from stem to stern again.

The roustabouts were in the huddle demanded of them. The Negro was not among them. Their close grouping enabled three of the riflemen to cover them.

'I asked what you want?' McBride roared from the wheelhouse.

'Every cent you got aboard,' came the reply. 'Eight of my men'll collect. Be as scared as you folks when they come aboard.' His head swung from side to side, to ensure that every passenger and crewman saw the grim determination in his eyes. 'Least sign of trouble, they'll start blasting. Get blown up with the boat same as you folks. But willing to take the risk.' He waved the dynamite towards the huddle of roustabouts. 'Anyone happens to go on living, won't ever sleep much after seeing these men get it.'

He gave a low-voiced order and eight of the riflemen advanced, away from the horses. They split into two groups of four and divided to board by separate gangplanks.

'Hear this!' McBride yelled. 'To the passengers and crew of my ship. There is to be no resistance! I repeat, no resistance!'

Many voices spoke softly, all of them contributing to an angry and fearful mumble. The man with the dynamite struck the second match and watched it flare. The talk was abruptly curtailed and the match was dropped. Another was drawn from the pocket as the two groups of boarders came off the bowing gangplanks and their footfalls crunched the snow on the Main Deck.

The door of the woman's cabin was cracked open. 'Anything I can do, Captain?' Rhett asked anxiously.

'Get out here,' the half-breed told him. 'They find you inside with a woman they're sure to figure something's queer.'

Rhett opened the door just wide enough to allow him to slide out sideways. He closed it again and glowered at Edge.

'There are just so many cracks a man can take, Captain.'

Edge glanced sourly over his shoulder. 'No comment, feller.'

He returned his attention to the dock. With no trace of fear, the man with the dynamite and the three riflemen behind him continued to wait patiently: completely exposed and ready to commit wholesale slaughter. The eight members of the bunch who had come aboard subdivided again – into pairs. Four remained on the Main Deck while the other four climbed up to the Hurricane and Boiler Decks. Then the man on the Hurricane Deck was left on his own, his partner taking the stairway up on to the superstructure to head for the wheel-house.

'You don't think it's a straightforward raid, Captain?' Rhett asked, the whine of complaint gone from his voice. One of his hands was inside his topcoat and jacket, obviously fisted around the Apache Knuckle-duster. 'Or you just being over-cautious.'

Everyone – passengers and crew – were on the port side of the boat, having been drawn there by the killing of Fryer. Two riflemen advanced on to the companionway from the Boiler

Deck and one from the Hurricane Deck.

'Money?' the man approaching from forward demanded. He held his Winchester one-handed, stock pressed to his hip by an elbow. The hammer of the rifle was cocked. His free hand was extended. He looked cold and tired and breathless, the expelled air from his lungs billowing like steam as it forced exit through his clenched teeth.

Rhett hesitated, waiting for a lead from Edge. The half-breed dug into his hip pocket, leaning forward slightly to conceal the bulge of the shotgun. Behind them, the two men were making similar demands from other passengers.

'One shot and all hell will be broke loose!' the man with the dynamite warned.

'I told you people!' McBride augmented.

Edge put his bankroll into the man's hand. It was pocketed and the hand extended to accept Rhett's money. His roll was bigger, bulked by the five hundred dollar advance Ferris had given him.

'It sure isn't like I thought it would be,' Rhett muttered bitterly. 'Bob wrote you never allowed anybody to – '

'Open that door!' the rifleman ordered after he had put the second roll of bills into his pocket. 'We gotta check everywhere.'

'Not in the war, feller,' Edge replied conversationally. 'Nor in Omaha.'

Rhett gave a curt nod of understanding. His hand remained under his coats, gripping the combination revolver, knife and knuckle-duster. The rifleman did not see the signal of acknowledgement and Rhett continued to watch Edge closely, but not pointedly.

Further along the companionway, the two men who had come aboard at the stern were robbing the other cabin passengers and getting no resistance.

Edge opened the door of Ferris's cabin and stepped aside. He saw the grey-haired, overweight occupant standing by the bed, still in his nightshirt. The rifleman showed no reluctance in putting his back towards Edge and Rhett as he stepped across the threshold. He used the heel of a boot to kick the door closed.

'Feller wants a cut of what you got,' Edge said quickly, his face impassive as he looked across the rifleman's shoulder just before the door closed.

And it never did close, because Edge put his boot against

84

the base of the frame. The door hit the side of his boot and bounced open – to crash into the back of the rifleman. The man started to turn in surprise and fear. Which gave Horace Ferris the time he needed to bring the knife from behind him and hurl it. Although the nightshirted man lacked speed, he possessed power and accuracy with his throwing arm.

The knife sank deep into the rifleman's chest, left of centre. He was starting to fall, the Winchester already loosed by dead fingers, as Edge gripped the handle of the swinging door and pulled it closed. He caught a brief glimpse of the face of Ferris: expressing a mixture of fear, satisfaction and pride.

Rhett grinned fleetingly. 'What now, Captain?'

'Silence is golden, feller,' Edge replied softly as the two men from the stern halted outside the door of the woman's cabin. 'Noise could be leaden.'

'Anyone inside?' one of the riflemen demanded.

The other divided his suspicious attention between the half-breed and Rhett and the passengers at the other end of the companionway.

'I'm not decent!' Charity called shrilly.

'Just your money we want, lady,' the spokesman for the pair growled, and pushed open the door. He expressed disappointment. 'You got all the best parts covered.'

He stepped across the threshold. The other one remained outside. The voices of Charity and the rifleman contributed to a low mumble. On the deck above the cabins, footfalls crunched on crusted snow.

The sun burned a hole through the cloud cover above south-eastern Iowa. It was the colour of fresh spilled blood: a complete disc, clear of the horizon.

Down on the dock, the trio of riflemen and their dynamite-toting leader were as patiently unruffled as ever. Only the horses moved, scratching at the snow to try to locate grass. But there was only hard-packed dirt below, frozen solid.

The rifleman emerged from Charity's cabin, stuffing some money into his pocket. Edge tugged at the lobe of his right ear. Rhett was confused for a moment, unsure whether or not it was a signal and, if it was, what it implied. Then he recalled the itch which the half-breed had developed before claiming a hostage at the shipping company office in Omaha. Rhett became visibly tense.

'Where's Clay?' the spokesman for the two riflemen asked.

Edge hooked the thumb of his free hand and jerked it at the door to Ferris's cabin.

'Back off, both of you.'

One Winchester was aimed at Edge, the other at Rhett. The two went to the rail.

'How you doin'?' This from the man who had come below from the wheel-house and was approaching from the Hurricane Deck.

'Gonna give Clay a hand. I think maybe we've got what we came for.'

The man at the cabin entrance sloped the Winchester to his shoulder and used his free hand to turn the handle and push the door. It swung open without hitting any obstruction. The two men who remained outside glanced down at the dock. So did Edge.

They saw that the man with the dynamite was looking up at the companionway, as ready as ever to strike the match. The three guards continued to aim their rifles steadily at the roustabout hostages.

'Where's Clay?' the rifleman at the doorway snarled, starting to whip his Winchester down.

The riflemen outside craned their necks to see past the one in the doorway: to look at Horace Ferris, still in his nightshirt, and near the rumpled bed, both hands behind his back.

Edge groaned, loud and dramatically. He pushed his right hand under his coat, between two fastened buttons at his chest. His back slid down the rail palings as his feet slithered on the snow covering the deck.

'Captain?' Rhett yelled, his voice high with concern.

Ferris's fear expanded.

'Feint,' the half-breed rasped as his back hit the deck. 'With an *e*.'

All the riflemen had snapped their heads around to stare at the collapsing half-breed. For a moment, they were simply startled. Then suspicion became uppermost – as they saw the apparently prostrate man fold up his knees and raise his back from the companionway, his weight braced on his shoulders.

'Ben!' the man in the cabin doorway shrieked.

He and the other two swung their rifles towards Edge and Rhett.

The half-breed canted his knees to one side and squeezed one trigger of the shotgun. The rifleman on the left was lifted off his feet and tossed hard against the cabin bulkhead. Death showed as a look of grotesque ugliness on his pale face. The cause of his death was even more monstrous to witness: a deep crater in his abdomen – the crimson of blood speckled with the dark spots of the damaging leadshot, flanked by the pure whiteness of the exposed hip-bones. All of it apparently frozen until the corpse crashed into the bulkhead. Then the stomach and intestines spewed out: a pulpy ball with slimy tentacles that spattered to the trampled snow, to be hidden a half second later when the man with a hole in his middle fell to cover his displaced insides.

The other two riflemen on the companionway died at the same moment.

The one in the cabin doorway took the knife of Ferris in his back. He took two forward steps, short and inelegant, then dropped his rifle and reached behind him with both hands to try to grip the knife. The strength went from his legs and he dropped hard to his knees and tipped forward.

Rhett killed the third with the revolver action of his combination weapon, using the Apache Knuckle-duster with the same degree of speed and skill he had displayed at the card-table. The man took the bullet in his right eye, staggered backwards with a shrill scream and fell across the other two men as they went down. He was silenced by death before he was still.

'They sure did more than faint with an *a*, Captain!' Rhett yelled, with a grin pasted to his handsome face.

Edge had already grabbed one of the discarded Winchesters and was rolling over on to his stomach, the unyielding wood and metal of the shotgun digging painfully into his belly and chest. His hooded eyes, narrowed to glinting slits in the sunlight reflected on snow, saw a match flare.

'We ain't finished yet, feller,' he growled against a background of screams and shouts. 'Take a spell later.'

CHAPTER EIGHT

Rage carved deep lines into the face of the leader of the bunch. As he touched the match to the fuse of the dynamite, the expression that contorted his features was even more starkly displayed in the sparkling light of the hissing flame.

Camly, Edge took aim: resting the barrel of the Winchester on the lip of the deck, angling it down at his target.

Gunfire crackled.

On the wharf, three of the roustabouts crumpled, adding new bloodstains to the snow.

On the Main Deck of the *Delta Dawn*, one of the raiders put a bullet into the heart of an elderly woman passenger. Then he whirled to race for the stern gangplank. His three companions tried to escape without wasting time on personal retaliation.

All four of them could see the spluttering fuse burning towards the bundle of dynamite as their leader raised his arm to begin the throw.

On one knee, Rhett fired a hurriedly picked-up Winchester. One of the guards on the hostages was flipped over backwards, blood squeezing through the fingers of his hands as he covered his face. The other two, caught in the process of pumping the lever actions of their repeaters, were smashed to the ground by an assault of hurled logs and then the weight of the attacking roustabouts.

The dynamite sticks were released by the swinging arm: hurled in a graceful arc through the sun-bright air.

Edge angled the Winchester skywards between two of the rail palings. The muzzle tracked the bundle, caught up with it, and moved ahead. The brown-skinned finger squeezed the trigger.

Rhett fired his rifle a second time: and his bullet drilled a hole through the hard-packed snow where the leader of the bunch had been standing a moment before. The man had whirled, drawn his Colt and dived for the cover of the log pile.

On the Main Deck, two raiders were shot in the back by passengers and crewmen before they reached the gangplanks.

The dynamite exploded.

In wide, totally unconfined mid-air, the report was crashingly loud: but the noise quickly rolled out on all sides like fading thunder. The blast, too, had ample space in every direction to spread its force: except downwards. As the flare of the detonated explosive outshone the new sun for an instant, the attacking roustabouts were pushed harder on to their companions and the struggling riflemen beneath them. The bodies of the dead were driven through the snow to the frozen ground. The snow melted to water and froze to clear ice. The log pile crashed over to bury the man who had thrown the dynamite. Horses tumbled, struggled upright, and bolted.

The *Delta Dawn* canted towards mid-river, then was righted by the tautness of the mooring lines. All aboard who had not thrown themselves to the deck when the shooting started were hurled down by the forceful rush of air. Anything standing free and not heavy enough to withstand the blast was picked up and tossed.

The sound of the explosion and the chain reaction of noise it started was abruptly curtailed. Water rippled along the hull of the stern-wheeler. Steam hissed from her safety valves. Ears, recovered from the deafening effect of the explosion, heard only these familiar sounds: for thick snow muted the beat of galloping hooves.

'The South will rise again!' a man yelled.

The gangplanks had been dislodged by the blast. The man who had shrieked the promise leapt six feet of clear water at the bow and sprinted across the dock.

Edge, his hat whipped off by the blast, raked the Winchester around, pumping the action. With the same calmness that he had taken aim at the dynamite, he tracked the running man in his sights and squeezed the trigger again.

'You sure won't, feller,' he muttered as his bullet drilled a neat hole in the side of the man's head. The exit hole on the far side was not neat, made large and ragged by splinters of skull bone. Fragments of his blood-soaked brain stained the ground before his body crumpled and became still.

Women screamed and men shouted: the noise a mixture of jubilation, anger and hatred.

'Hold off!' a man's voice bellowed from the aft Main Deck. 'Some of you people are Southerners!'

'Quiet!' McBride roared from topside of the superstructure. 'I want a report from every section of my ship!'

Edge scrambled to his feet, unbuttoning his tattered coat and wrenching the shotgun out from his belt. He saw that his pants legs at about knee level were also holed and black. The skin had been broken beneath and he felt the sting of the wounds as he straightened.

'You changed your mind about the silence, uh Captain?' Rhett asked as Ferris and Charity came gingerly to the thresholds of their cabins. The woman had dressed to the extent of wearing a petticoat which left the upper spheres of her breasts and her shoulders bare but covered her decently elsewhere. She held her dress in one hand and a threaded needle in the other.

'Ain't just women allowed to alter their ideas, feller,' the half-breed growled, dragging his gaze away from the naked flesh of Charity's upper torso.

He snatched up his hat, jammed it on his head and swung a leg over the deck rail.

'Nobody died because I did!' the woman flung at him, then crashed the door closed.

'You took no for an answer?' Rhett asked, genuinely surprised, as the half-breed pulled his other leg over the rail.

'Shipboard romances never last,' Edge growled with a cold grin, holding on to the rail with one hand as he crouched, then dropping his legs and kicking them forward.

The momentum of the kick took him out of the vertical fall and he landed on the companionway of the Main Deck.

As above, several passengers stood or wandered about in a state of dazed shock. Crew members who had heard McBride's command scurried among the passengers or crouched beside the dead. But this activity was confined to the fore part of the deck. On the stern companionway, the sole survivor of the raiders was in a half crouch, rifle aimed from the shoulder towards a tight-knit group of fearful and confused passengers and crew. He had backed off as far as he could go before stepping out on to the wheel support.

'I'll surrender,' he was saying, his tongue continually darting out to moisten his trembling lips. 'To Southerners ready to follow the Cause again. This was no real robbery. Won't any of you people give me your word I'll be safe if I surrender?

I'll tell the whole story. It wasn't supposed to – '

Edge had advanced on the rear of the group. Close to it, he saw that several men had handguns clasped in their fists: many with clear shots available. He could not see their faces, but their stances and the way they craned their heads forward revealed the fascinated interest they had for what the rifleman was saying.

'Put up the gun, son,' a man urged. 'Maybe your boss would try to blow up innocent folks, but ain't everyone that's a savage.'

Edge could not get a clear shot at the rifleman without tipping his hand by showing the Winchester above the heads of the group. He grimaced at the memory of his Remington splashing into the river last night.

'I want an assurance!' the rifleman demanded. 'I want the Captain down here to give it to me.' Tears hung in the corners of his eyes. He looked suddenly very young.

'Go get McBride!' a woman snapped.

'I ain't shot no one,' the rifleman pleaded. 'Some of you people must have seen I didn't shoot no one.'

'Sure, son. Put up the gun before you do, uh?'

A shake of the head that flung the tears clear of his eyes. 'I'm not gonna trust no one 'cept the Captain.'

Nobody had complied with the woman's order. She was at the front of the group. She whirled, her wrinkled and care-worn face set in hard lines. The group parted to allow her passage. Edge moved only slightly and she had to swerve around him.

'Body wants somethin' done, best she does it herself!' she muttered with an angry glare at the half-breed.

'Or himself, ma'am,' Edge added, and fired from the hip, the Winchester barrel angled slightly upwards.

The group had not quite re-formed into a whole again after dividing to allow the woman to get through. The bullet spun along the narrowing gap and struck the rifleman in the chest. He groaned once, staggered backwards, dropped his Winchester and hit the paddle-wheel. The gap was wide again by the time he had bounced off the wheel and plunged into the ice-cold water between the boat and the wharf pilings.

'You killed him!' the man who had shared most of the exchanges with the raider accused.

His and many other guns were swung towards the impassive Edge as the whole group whirled to stare at him. The half-breed pumped the lever action of the rifle and continued to aim it between the divided group, pointing at no human target.

'What ails him don't have to be catching,' he muttered, shifting his glinting eyed gaze over the pale, cold-pinched faces which directed mass revulsion towards him.

'It appears to have reached epidemic proportions already!' another male member of the group said in a whining tone.

'They started to give us the treatment,' the half-breed answered wryly, and showed a cold grin as he heard McBride's angry voice behind him. He canted the rifle up to his shoulder. 'But the old kill or cure remedy worked in the end.'

'Who fired that shot?' the *Delta Dawn*'s master demanded, his bulky frame quaking with rage as he half ran along the companionway.

'He did!' This from the woman who had found it un-necessary to go for McBride. Her hand was rock steady as she pointed an accusing finger at Edge.

The uniformed man glowered hard into the unmoving face of the half-breed. 'You better have had good reason, mister!' he snarled. 'That's all I can say.'

There was a large group of passengers behind McBride. Most of them expressed shock or disgust. Rhett was among them, but he wore an expression of satisfaction. So was Horace Ferris, a top coat cloaking his nightshirt, and a pleading look on his face. Charity Meagher was at the forefront, her pretty features constantly changing their lines: never forming into an expression far removed from the brink of hysteria.

'I figure I got one, feller,' Edge replied. 'But it's a secret.'

'You'll tell me, mister!' McBride snarled in response. 'The authorities will need to know every last detail of this incident!'

'Except one, I figure,' Edge replied evenly, and dug for the makings in his shirt-pocket, his eyes ignoring the boat's master to concentrate on Charity Meagher. Her body was fully protected from the cold and male eyes now, by the blue dress with the white lace trimmings. The needle and thread had been left in the cabin and no fresh stitching showed on the silken fabric. 'That's already sewn up.'

CHAPTER NINE

'Was it a guess, Captain?' Henry Rhett asked.

'What, feller?'

'That the raid was a blind. You knew from the start it was really Ferris and the letter they were after.'

The two men sat at a table in the main salon, a bottle of whisky between them and a glass each in front of them. They were alone except for a bartender, and four stewards who waited idly beside tables laid for breakfast which nobody wanted.

Out in the timber behind the wharf, roustabouts were working up a sweat in the early morning cold: digging graves for the dead. All twelve raiders had died, along with three roustabouts and one woman passenger. Two additional graves were dug into the frozen ground – for the would-be assassin Rhett had killed at the poker table, and for Fryer, the wood-cutter.

The *Delta Dawn*'s complement of crew did not include a doctor, but there was an army surgeon bound for Fort Sully travelling as a passenger. And he was treating the wounded in a commandeered cabin: three men with minor injuries from blast and four women suffering from shock.

From time to time, passengers made to enter the salon for breakfast: but saw Edge and quickly turned away. It was obvious that a report of the final shot to be fired in the battle – and perhaps even the story that the half-breed had instigated the gun-battle – had been circulated around the stern-wheeler. Whichever, no one who had hurriedly reclaimed his or her stolen money from the bodies of the raiders appeared to regard Edge's actions favourably.

'They were too full of the God-on-our-side bullshit to be just hold-up men, feller. You ought to have spotted that.'

Rhett grimaced and took a gulp of whisky. 'I told you, Captain. I'm strictly an amateur in that line. Same as that bitch Jason. And that butch bastard Scott. What you mean, Captain? God-on-our – '

'Amateurs, like you,' Edge cut in, and sipped the rye with relish, the alcohol taking the taste of gunsmoke out of his mouth. 'But with their tails in the air for a different reason. Men need a better reason than money to put their lives on the line the way they did.'

'Just that? You figured they figured themselves as big heroes for the Cause just because they took risks?'

Edge grinned coldly, took another drink and rasped the back of a hand over his jaw bristles. 'Only one of them died before I was sure, feller. The one that stole my money.'

The half-breed had his money back in his hip pocket now. Down on the Main Deck, Ferris had pushed free of the crowd and made McBride the promise that he could explain Edge's actions. The *Delta Dawn*'s master had accepted this, still angry, and confined his parting snarl at Edge to a warning that he was not to leave the stern-wheeler.

Ferris was with McBride now.

Charity had rushed back to her cabin, still maintaining the pretense to all except a few that she had no connection with Ferris.

Edge had come directly to the salon, stopping only once, to retrieve his stolen money from the corpse behind the door of Ferris's cabin. Rhett had come hard on his heels.

'I can see why you weren't absolutely sure, Captain,' the man across the table from the half-breed muttered. 'Seeing how you risked your own and a lot of other people's lives for money. They could have been like you.'

'Don't claim to be unique.'

Rhett nodded, then shook his head. 'Bob wrote me a lot about you and I've seen you operate, Captain. But I guess I'll never understand you.'

Edge emptied his glass and showed a wry grin as the liquor burned down his throat. 'Your brother never did, that's for sure.'

'Not for want of trying.'

'Yeah. He never stopped trying to get to the bottom of every man.'

'Go to hell!' Rhett snarled, and lunged upright, his knees banging the underside of the table.

Edge was holding his glass and he fisted a hand around the bottle before it could tip.

'Can't you ever be serious with me?'

Rhett had spun around and started for the door, his mincing, hip-swaying gait accentuated by the rage. His lips pouted girlishly as he flung the question back over his shoulder.

'Told you once, feller,' Edge growled. 'Not even just good friends.'

Earlier, Charity Meagher had slammed a door in Edge's face. Now Henry Rhett did it, at longer range but with more violent temper.

'Is he what I think he is?' a dour-faced steward asked, trying to mask the depth of his interest.

'It sure ain't just the way he walks,' Edge answered, poured himself another drink, rose, and carried the brimful glass and the Winchester to a table set for breakfast. 'Anything that's filling,' he told the steward closest to him. 'And hot coffee.'

The man scooted away, pleased to have something to occupy his time. The bartender came out from behind his counter to retrieve the bottle. One steward polished cutlery on a cloth and the other two attended to the fire in the pot-bellied stove.

Echoes of war sounded in the half-breed's mind. There had been a lot of men suffering a great deal of boredom then, between the battles and skirmishes that presented the opportunities to kill or be killed. And there had been men, of higher status, who discussed situations and took decisions in remote places: removed from the arenas of war. And still other men who acted on the very borderline between life and death — these actions risking the lives of others as much as their own.

As in the war, Edge experienced no agony of remorse about the three roustabouts and the woman passenger who were being lowered into the frozen ground because he had taken the action he did. The twelve raiders were going into the same ground, every cent of stolen money had been recovered, the *Delta Dawn* was still in one piece — and Ferris and the letter were safe.

The Union was not in a state of war with the Confederacy: but to prevent a war was as important as to win one. The enemy had dictated that the methods of achieving the former should be the same as the latter objective.

Edge ate his breakfast with an untroubled mind. He compared Charity Meagher with Jeannie Fisher, Henry Rhett with his brother, Ferris and McBride with senior army officers he had experienced, the passengers and crew of the stern-wheeler

95

with nameless and faceless troopers and himself with Captain Josiah C. Hedges.

In almost all cases, the echoes were distorted. In one respect, they were not. Hedges had been his own man forced by circumstances to rely on the help of others. So was Edge.

Breakfast was good, except for the second cup of coffee he drank after he had finished eating. It came from the same pot as the first, but it tasted bitter. But it was not the sourness in his mouth that carved the lines of a grimace on to his lean, dark-skinned face. Just his thought process, until his mind carried him out of the stove-heated salon to the memory of being alone on the blizzard-ravaged deck in the darkness: surrounded by potential danger and keyed up to meet it.

The door of the salon swung open.

Instinctively, Edge dropped a hand to grasp the frame of the Winchester leaning against his chair.

Horace Ferris entered first, freshly washed up and shaved and warmly dressed against the cold weather outside. Rhett and Charity Meagher were immediately behind him: as freshly turned out to experience the new day as was the New Orleans businessman.

'Captain McBride has ordered the entire crew ashore for the interment service,' Ferris announced solemnly. 'Passengers are at liberty to choose.'

The bartender and stewards grinned their welcome of the news, and hurried out, shrugging on their topcoats and eager to enjoy a break in the dull routine that had existed since the raid.

Rhett shut the door in their wake and then followed Ferris and Charity to the table where Edge sat. The two men smelled of pomade and the woman of a more subtle perfume. All three expressed a kind of grim solemnity which obviously had nothing to do with the mass funeral about to take place on the snow-covered bank of the river.

'I have told McBride of our mission in general,' Ferris said.

He sat opposite Edge. Charity was at the end of the table. Rhett remained standing.

'How general?' the half-breed asked.

'That we are on important Government business and that forces seeking to overthrow the Government are attempting to stop us. I did not mention the document or the fact that I intend to hand it directly to the President.' He was starting to sweat in the warmth of the salon. Beads of moisture oozed

96

out of his thinning hairline and trickled down his forehead. He mopped at them with a pure white handkerchief before they dripped off his brow.

'The man is no fool, Edge. And there is probably nobody dense enough aboard this ship not to realise that the attempted robbery had a political motive.'

Edge nodded, stood up and ambled to a window. Morning was well advanced now, the sun high and bright. The snow on the ground was dazzlingly white. The crowd of crewmen and passengers gathered around the area of open graves was swelling by the moment. The bodies were already in their final resting places. McBride stood alone in the centre of the embryo cemetery, a bible protruding from a pocket as he blew visible breath into his cupped hands.

'Left them cold, uh?'

'McBride has not yet confirmed the suspicions of the rest. Although I could not be specific and was unable to show him proof of our intent, I think he believes me. But he claims that his position as master of the *Delta Dawn* means he must be neutral. That the safety of his ship and her passengers and crew is his prime concern.'

'That is traditional,' Charity put in tautly.

'Tradition is the main obstacle to progress,' Rhett muttered. 'That's said a lot.'

'Tradition of burying the dead is sure holding us up,' the half-breed augmented.

McBride had opened the bible now and every man at the graves had removed his hat. The captain's words did not carry as far as the salon.

'But he is prepared to put it to a democratic vote,' Ferris continued, his tone betraying irritation at the interruption. 'After the interment, he will take advantage of having the ship's company and the passengers gathered together. He will tell them what I told him and ask them to choose whether we should be allowed to continue as passengers.'

Charity vented an unladylike snort of disgust. 'Adding there is always the risk that the Rebels will strike again, with little regard for the lives of the innocent!'

Edge glanced over his shoulder towards the table. He saw that the woman's chagrin was directed entirely at the older man. Ferris attempted to cover one of her hands with his own. But she snatched her arm back quickly. Ferris looked hurt, then stared earnestly at Edge's back.

'I appreciate that you acted in the interest of our mission this morning. Having taken part in the killing myself, I obviously condone what you did. But I cannot allow innocent lives to be put at risk in the future – unless those in danger are aware of the situation. I therefore intend to abide by the will of the majority.'

He sighed deeply, as if intensely relieved to have stated his views.

Edge continued to look out at the funeral, as he struck a match on the bulkhead and lit a just rolled cigarette.

'We're gonna get off this boat and walk if that's the way the vote goes?' he asked evenly.

'We will disembark, certainly,' Ferris confirmed pompously. 'The horses of the Rebels will not have scattered far in these weather conditions. Indeed, it may well be advantageous to leave this ship and travel by another means – unknown to the enemies of the Union.'

There was a long silence inside the salon. Outside, at the rear of the dock, McBride snapped the bible closed and put his uniform cap back on his head. Roustabouts moved forward, to begin shovelling displaced earth back into the graves. But McBride shouted and held up his hands, to recapture attention again.

'What do you think, Edge?' Charity asked.

'It is immaterial!' Ferris said firmly. 'I am in charge of this mission. I welcome help, whether the reason it is given me be patriotism or financial reward. But I am prepared to complete it alone if needs be. Mr Edge, Mr Rhett or you, my dear, may certainly remain aboard the *Delta Dawn* if any of you feel so inclined.'

Out on the burial ground, McBride was making a speech. Interest, rather than a sense of duty, ensured he held the attention of his audience this time. Edge put his back to the scene.

'I'm with you, Captain,' Rhett said eagerly.

The half-breed curled back his lips to display his teeth: very white against the darkness of his bristles. 'Got no objection to that, feller. When we've got our backs to the wall.'

Rhett showed a much warmer grin than that of the half-breed. 'I don't like it, but I'll take it – from you.'

Despite Charity's disenchantment with Ferris, it was obvious the new turn of events had not cancelled out her ill-feeling

98

towards Edge. But the half-breed was certain she would go along with his opinion.

He wrinkled his nose, as if he had caught a bad odour on the stove-heated air.

'Is that your response?' Charity snapped.

'Just seeing if that kind smells, lady,' he answered.

'Kind? Of what?' The colour that filled her cheeks was created by impatience now.

'Bullshit.' He glanced over his shoulder as Ferris made a spluttering noise.

McBride had put the proposition to his audience and no more than half a dozen had raised their hands. As Edge's narrowed eyes located the scene, these hands were lowered. McBride said a single word and many more arms were thrust skywards. The master of the *Delta Dawn* showed a smile of relief and waved for the roustabouts to fill in the graves as he started back for his boat.

'Sir, I resent – ' Ferris started.

Edge swung his head and fixed the man with a stare that was colder than the outside temperature. He pumped the action of the Winchester. Ferris expressed fear. Rhett brightened his grin and Charity showed satisfaction.

'Ain't no democracy in war time, feller,' the half-breed muttered. 'We just lost the vote. But I ain't about to concede anything.'

Ferris started to rise.

'Rhett!' Edge snapped.

'Captain?'

'If he tries for the knife, kill him!'

Charity gasped.

'Will do!' Rhett acknowledged, levelling, cocking and aiming his rifle.

Edge went to the door, jerked it open, threw the stock of the Winchester to his shoulder and squeezed the trigger. Yells and screams accompanied the gunshot. The bullet kicked up snow a foot in front of McBride. The man halted abruptly. His, and every other head on shore swung towards the tall, rock-steady, almost statue-like figure of the half-breed at the deck rail. Some of the shocked eyes blinked as sunlight glinted on the rifle-barrel.

'You people want some more of hell froze over?' Edge shouted.

'Ferris agreed to abide by the wish of – '

'That was between you and him!' Edge cut in. 'Awhile back. He ain't very agreeable at all, right now.'

'We can rush 'em, Mr McBride!' a man on one side of the crowd suggested, his voice tremoring with excitement or fear.

Edge turned from the waist, elevated his aim and squeezed the trigger. The man who had yelled vented a howl and the Winchester was back covering McBride by the time the displaced hat scaled to the snow.

'Just a hat!' Edge snarled at the shocked crowd. 'Anyone want to bring matters to a head?'

The threat erupted screams and gasps, then brought silence.

'What is it you want?' McBride demanded at length. 'My ship?'

'Already got that. Vote wasn't unanimous.'

The big Negro – Linn – was the first to elbow his way clear of the crowd and swing wide of McBride to approach the forward gangplank.

'Stinkin' nigger!' an unidentified voice yelled.

'Boy, the North-South trouble ain't just about abolition!' another man called.

Linn halted halfway across the gangplank. Six other men broke from the crowd to trail him.

'Maybe so!' the big black man drawled. 'But it sure is the only bit I give a shit about.'

The men trailing him were viewed with mass contempt by the crowd they had left. Four of them were crew members and the other two passengers. Edge knew that at least one – perhaps two – had not voted in favour of aiding and abetting Ferris.

'All you people are guilty of serious crimes!' McBride shouted. 'Mutiny or piracy!'

'And perhaps even murder!' a woman added shrilly. 'We could all perish left here without food and hardly any shelter.'

'Nonsense!' Charity Meagher countered as she stepped from the salon doorway. 'With the blizzard over there'll be many boats passing shortly.'

'Hey, up there! We got 'em covered real good.'

Edge canted the Winchester to his shoulder and leaned over the rail to look down at the Main Deck. The six white men were positioned at regular intervals along the lower deck rail. All of them had claimed a Winchester from the pile of weapons taken from the dead raiders. They aimed the rifles

100

out towards the group behind the dock. Linn was standing at the bow cleat:

'I want to get off!' This was a short, fat man who waddled to the stern gangplank. 'Is it all right if I get off? Me and my ladyfr . . . me and my lady wife?'

He had a bald head that glistened with the sweat of fear. The woman who trailed tentatively behind him was thin, sour-faced and twice his age. Her complexion was beet red.

'Please, we don't want to get involved!' the woman called up towards Edge.

'I don't have to like your choice, feller,' the half-breed answered wryly. 'But you can get it off with whoever you like.'

The couple scuttled out across the gangplank. Edge redirected his attention to the riflemen below him.

'You fellers can run this boat?'

'No sweat, suh!' Linn confirmed.

'So do it. You won't get any hassle.'

He straightened and tipped the Winchester forward again, bringing up his free hand to steady his aim at McBride. Something brushed his elbow and he shot a sidelong glance at the woman. She was aiming Rhett's Winchester in the same manner, grimacing at the weight of the gun.

'It's all right,' she rasped. 'Mr Ferris has a knife at his throat.'

'Puts him in a hell of a lot more danger than the people down there,' the half-breed muttered.

'They don't know that,' she countered stiffly.

Steam hissed from the safety valves with urgency for the first time since the late night docking. And the engines rumbled with the drive still disengaged.

'You won't get far without a pilot!' McBride snarled. 'And if snags don't stop you, I'll make sure the authorities do.'

'Cast off forward!' Linn shouted from the wheel-house. 'Cast off the sternline!'

'I don't like it,' Charity muttered.

'It didn't show – the first time.'

She snorted, unladylike again. 'I mean the way they're taking it so calmly. You'd think – '

'I think not too many people take guns to a funeral,' Edge cut in. 'I think most of them are scared. I think maybe there are just a handful of them feel strong enough to join in another war.'

The lines had been released and the gangplanks hauled

aboard. Black smoke was billowing from the twin stacks. The *Delta Dawn* drifted away from the wharf and downstream on the Missouri current. Drive was engaged and the paddle-wheel began to thrash the water. Her rudders were held hard over and she nosed out further towards mid-river and began to make way.

Edge lowered his rifle and the woman imitated him, with a sigh of relief. She sagged against the rail.

'There are women and old people here!' McBride roared, turning towards the crowd as they made to surge forward. He threw his hands high in the air and his voice and the gesture halted the rush. 'Men more able than us will see those people get their just desserts!'

'McBride is right, Edge!' Horace Ferris snarled as he was urged across the salon threshold by Rhett's pressure – the blade part of the combination weapon held against the nape of his neck. 'You have committed piracy and incited mutiny. Most serious crimes at a time when a state of war does not exist.'

'Same brand of bullshit as before, uh Captain?' Rhett asked. 'Just because there hasn't been any big battles, that doesn't mean we aren't in a war of some kind.'

The sun continued to shine down brightly as it touched its mid-morning position against the eastern dome of the sky. The air, again given an illusion of movement by the forward progress of the boat, seemed to penetrate clothing and flesh to chill deep-buried bones. Ice-floes started to crunch against the stern-wheeler's spoon bow again. Nebraska and Iowa were covered with a deep layer of crusted snow for as far as the eye could see.

Edge jerked his hat brim lower over his forehead, turned up the collar of his coat and held the rifle in the crook of his right arm so he could push his hands into his pockets.

'If it is, feller,' he muttered, 'it sure is a cold war.'

CHAPTER TEN

The *Delta Dawn* made good time away from the stranded crew and passengers at the fuel stop. The two passengers who had chosen to continue north aboard the stern-wheeler elected to fire the boilers. Both were young, and strong from the rigours of silver mining, which was their trade. Linn and the ship's cook shared the first period of duty in the wheel-house and the only man handling his own job was an engineer. The other two men, together with Edge and Rhett, divided their time around the boat, learning what was necessary for when the watches changed.

Charity Meagher and a subdued Horace Ferris kept busy in the galley, preparing the midday meal.

Presented with the *fait accompli* of the confiscated boat, Ferris acknowledged that lack of co-operation could only harm his aim. He had his knife returned to him and, like everyone else aboard, was hardly ever without, and always within easy reach of, a rifle or revolver.

The weather remained bright and bitterly cold, the sun being the only blemish on the otherwise solid blue of the sky. There was no wind and the Missouri flowed evenly – muddy brown except for the clear bow-waves and white wakes of boat traffic.

As morning grew old, noon was overtaken and the afternoon progressed, every kind of craft showed on the wide waterway. Stern-wheelers, side-wheelers, yawls, mackinaws, keelboats, flatboats, rowboats and dugout canoes travelled both north and south. The *Delta Dawn* often swung wide with the skilful handling of the Negro to pass other north-bound boats. Always to leave them far behind in quick time, her boilers roaring, her engines whining and her wheel thudding.

The broadly grinning Linn, immensely enjoying his role as token master, always ignored the enraged shouts and violently shaken fists that were directed towards his wheel-house as other craft underway were pitched and rolled in the thrashing, foaming water swirled up by the rapidly-turning wheel.

Once everybody aboard, with the exception of Charity and Ferris, was familiar with the intricacies of the boilers, engines and steering gear, off-duty men either slept or kept watch on the banks. This careful surveillance of Nebraska and Iowa was maintained from the superstructure each side of the wheelhouse: the man inside who was not on the helm having to concentrate his attention on the river immediately ahead – searching for ice-floes and snags that could rip the bottom out of the racing stern-wheeler, sandspits which could ground her or lesser obstructions which were a risk to the twin rudders and paddle-wheel.

Edge was watching the Iowa side of the river when Charity came up the stairway from the Hurricane Deck, two mugs of steaming coffee in either hand. She gave one to Rhett who was watching the Nebraska bank, handed two into the wheelhouse and then squatted down beside the half-breed with the final one.

'It's too easy, isn't it?' she asked nervously after watching him drink the fast-cooling coffee.

'It'll get tougher, ma'am.'

'I realise that.' She hugged herself, her arms forming bars against the coat-contoured mounds of her breasts. But there was no way to protect her face from the bite of the freezing air and her clear skin was bluish white. 'Mr Ferris feels the authorities are turning a blind eye to us. The people we left behind must have been rescued by now.'

Edge nodded as he continued to survey snow-covered Iowa. 'But first they got to get to a telegraph office. Closest one will be at Omaha.'

'Of course!' Charity exclaimed.

'And we ain't passed no town bigger than a couple of shacks so far. Maybe Sioux City has a telegraph office. I don't know.'

'Neither do I.'

The half-breed drained the mug, swallowed most of the coffee, and spat the grit-like grounds over the side. 'That might be the kind of information people would expect a secret agent to know,' he growled.

Charity didn't answer for long moments, until Edge directed a bleak-eyed glance at her. 'All right, you might as well be told. Mr Ferris and me are no more secret agents than you

104

are. He's just a New Orleans cotton man and – '

'Who just happens to be good with a throwing knife. A little slow maybe, but – '

'A skill he acquired as a child! One he used as a party trick until this started.'

'Sure beats pulling rabbits out of a hat.'

'And I am merely a school-teacher. But everything else we told you is true. There is a letter: and a group of Government agents in New Orleans did obtain it from the new Rebels.'

'Always did believe that, ma'am,' he told her, raking his hooded eyes back and forth along the river bank again. 'Wouldn't have done so much killing on a hunch.'

'It was that last man you shot which turned you against Mr Ferris, wasn't it?'

'You weren't exactly rooting for him for awhile, ma'am.'

'Because I disagreed with his decision. Although I despise killing, I realised you had to kill that man to salvage whatever shreds of secrecy are left with regard to our mission. Then Mr Ferris told Captain McBride almost everything.'

'Secret agent wouldn't have done that,' Edge pointed out wryly.

Charity sighed and her tone became melancholy. 'John Ferris worked for the Government, Edge. He was the son of Mr Ferris and the last member of the group to die. He gave the letter to his father and made him promise to deliver it personally to Mr Coolidge. I got there just as John died.'

'Why you, ma'am.'

'John and I were engaged to be married. He was the first, and the last man before you.'

When Edge glanced at her again, he saw she had learned to control her blushes. Her pretty face was still white tinged with blue.

'I said I'd help Mr Ferris. But when the Rebels caught up with us, we knew we'd have little chance of success on our own. And we didn't think anyone would help us unless we claimed official status. For we are doing this only partially from patriotism. Mostly, we feel we owe it to a man we both loved.'

The *Delta Dawn* steamed past a farmstead perched on a low bluff. A rowboat moored at a small wooden dock pitched crazily in the wash from the stern-wheel.

'You are helping for another consideration, Edge. Mr Ferris asked me to give you this.'

She thrust out a hand towards him. He looked at the stack

of ten dollar bills held against the palm by her thumb.

'Obliged,' he said, taking the money and pushing it into a side pocket of his coat.

'He also asked me to tell you he is sorry for his attitude during the confiscation of the *Delta Dawn*. He acknowledges that you were right to act in the way you did. And he offers you command of the mission.'

'Pay and conditions in this war are a hell of a lot better than the last one,' the half-breed muttered.

Charity stood up.

'You still have the letter, ma'am?'

She cupped her left breast, then pulled her hand away quickly when the ice-blue eyes looked up at her. 'Sewn into the bodice of my dress. May I keep it there?'

The thin lips curled back from the teeth. 'Ain't nowhere better to keep valuable property than in a fancy chest.'

Again, there was no colouring of her complexion. 'You're hurt, Edge.'

She was looking towards the hole in the lower part of his coat. Through this it was possible to see the tattered pants just above the knees and the congealed blood on the torn flesh below.

'I'll attend to it when it's your turn to rest, if you like?'

'Figure it'll only hurt if I kneel down, ma'am. Never yet got on my knees for anything.'

She started to form an angry frown, but controlled it. 'Perhaps when this is all over we could . . . could start from scratch.'

'We already did,' he told her. 'If it wasn't so cold I'd maybe show you what you did to my back – when it wasn't so cold.'

This time, her embarrassment was too great to control. Her entire face was bright scarlet. Then she whirled and went across the decking as fast as she could, her boots slithering on the hard-packed snow. Her vocal response was delayed: a howl as she went down the stairway to the Hurricane Deck.

Rhett's grinning face showed at the front of the wheel-house. 'Women can be a real pain in the ass, can't they, Captain?'

'How would you know that, feller?'

The other man continued to grin as he nodded. 'Right, how would I know that?'

'Watch the bank.'

'For what, Captain? There hasn't been time. Nobody knows.'

'Just do it, uh?'

The *Delta Dawn* ploughed upriver through the afternoon and into evening. There was no stop at Sioux City, where the Missouri swung north-west, to form a fork with the Vermilion River which continued on northwards. It was dusk then, the moon low and still weak. The lights from the town's crude buildings winked across the water and were reflected on its surface.

Edge had slept and shaved and eaten and was again on watch at the starboard side of the wheel-house. One of the roustabouts tending the boilers came up the stairway to report that the stock of cordwood was dangerously low. Men on the Sioux City dockside yelled and waved at the stern-wheeler as she steamed by, smoke billowing from her stacks and paddle turning at full speed.

The half-breed ignored the shore and told the roustabout he would order a halt at the first stand of timber that showed on either bank. The man was a middle-aged central-European with a strong accent. He was short and broad and strong, with a face that had been battered in many brawls. Edge trusted him. He also trusted the Negro, the two silver miners and a fair haired young steward. Which left two roustabouts he was unsure of. One elderly and fat with a drinker's belly and the other in his mid-twenties but with eyes that looked far older.

So far, the only caution he had shown towards these two was to ensure that they never had the same duty assignment.

After Sioux City, the river formed the boundary between Nebraska to the south and the Dakotas to the north. There was no visible change in the terrain – low, rolling country blanketed with almost solid whiteness. As the moon brightened, the temperature dropped. The currents lost their strength and a new sound became as constant as the thud of the engine, hiss of escaping steam and thrash of the paddles: the splinter of thin ice as the water began to freeze.

It was close to midnight when Linn opened a window in the wheel-house and pushed his head through as the mid-European roustabout came up the stairway to report that the fuel was all but exhausted.

A stand of fir trees grew tantalisingly close to the Dakota bank. But the way to a landing was barricaded by the snags of old, uprooted trees: their boughs protruding up through the water like the skeletonised limbs of countless dead men.

'We either get our keel ripped out or we get grounded, suh,' Linn told the pensive Edge. 'Or we could anchor out here and

107

use the yawl as a ferry. Take time, though. And I reckon we'd be froze solid before the chore was half done. We just gotta keep movin', suh.'

'Obliged,' the half-breed acknowledged. Then, to the roustabout from the boiler room. 'Do like the man says, feller. Keep moving.'

An angry frown showed on the battered face. 'Vhat vith? Ve need fuel.'

'Ten men and one woman aboard, feller. We don't need a boat big as this.' He rapped a fist on the side of the wheelhouse. 'Mostly built of timber, ain't she?'

The black and the white roustabout both grinned broadly.

'I vill get out the axes.'

'Do that, feller.'

The white crewman hurried down the stairway, still grinning. Linn vented a gust of laughter before withdrawing his head and banging the window shut.

'What's the joke, Captain?' Rhett asked, showing confusion as he appeared in front of the wheel-house.

'Choppers are coming out. Makes some fellers feel gay.'

CHAPTER ELEVEN

The stern-wheeler slid past Yankton and the mouth of the James River in the pre-dawn hours of the bitterly cold night. At sun-up the Niobrara could be seen snaking westwards between its snow-covered banks. The *Delta Dawn* turned to starboard to follow the course of the Missouri towards Fort Randall where she left the Nebraska line to head into the Dakotas.

Randall was a huddle of crude buildings: an army and trading post with a landing stage. A south-bound stern-wheeler was moored to the dock. Aboard her and on the shore, people stared in amazement at the *Delta Dawn*. For the churning riverboat was already stripped of much of her superfluous equipment and even as she sped beyond the small community men continued to swing sun-glinting axes into her woodwork.

Every rail had been removed, the forward spars and derricks were gone, all but a couple of her cabin doors were out of their frames, holds were minus their hatches and several areas of deck boarding had been torn up.

Wood smoke belching from the stacks now had the smell of burning pitch in it.

Laughter sounded from the shore, drowning the voices of those who yelled inquiries towards the *Delta Dawn*.

Every man not engaged with the boilers, engines or wheelhouse duty was wielding an axe and piling up heaps of timber. But all had a rifle close at hand. And, while ignoring the overt responses from the people on the shore, most kept careful watch for signs of trouble.

During the night, when the men had to work their hardest to rebuild a stock of fuel, Edge had become aware of mounting resentment – which had acted to dampen the enthusiasm which most of them had exhibited initially. Even Linn had started to mutter his disgruntlement: complaining he could not see the need for constant high speed and relentless vigilance.

And Rhett had growled: 'The way I heard it from Bob, Captain, you weren't always so close-mouthed. Used to tell your guys what you had in mind.'

Ferris had been in the forward hold with them, helping to smash open crates and chop the timber into boiler fuel. He answered for the taciturn half-breed.

'The quicker we get where we are going, the quicker the job will be done,' he explained breathlessly. 'And we have to keep careful watch for the enemy.'

'I know that, suh,' Linn croaked. 'But what enemy? Where? How they know where we are?'

'You know the enemy, mister. Rebels not ready to put on uniforms again yet. Since Omaha they've known we were aboard this ship. They have already made three attempts to stop us getting through. Two such attempts unrelated to the third. The news has been spread along the length of this river. With the enemy ahead never certain whether those on the lower reaches have succeeded in stopping us.

'And the fact that we are on a Government mission is common knowledge now. There will be no more subtle attempts because subterfuge is now pointless. Surprise would not be, of course.'

'Says it all, I guess,' Edge had acknowledged when Ferris looked at him.

'Except what the enemy's after, suh?' Linn posed.

'Kill us, feller. Ought to be enough to convince you and the rest to keep working and watching?'

'Ain't nothin' more important to a man than his own skin, suh,' Linn allowed. 'Be it black or white.' Then he grinned as Charity came into the hold with mugs of coffee. 'Or pretty. I'll spread the word around, suh.'

Later, Ferris and Edge had taken a break together, in a cabin fitted with four beds. Rhett and the fair-haired steward slept on the other two.

'I don't think the Rebels are working so haphazardly, Mr Edge,' the older man said through the cold darkness of one of the few cabins which still had a door.

'New Orleans is a big, tough city, I guess?'

'Yes.'

'The kind where a man doesn't get rich with just party-trick knife-throwing. He has to be smart.'

Ferris sighed. 'The attempt on my life during the poker game was well planned.'

110

'Execution was a little off.'

'Likewise when Edward Manx came aboard. And the raid at the fuel stop landing. The Rebels are hedging their bets. Every plan was laid before the first one was put into operation.'

'Learned from their mistakes in the last war, feller. But they ain't hindered by Robert E. Lee and Jeff Davis this time.'

'I fear that the closer we get to Fort Sully, the more stubborn their final line of defence will be.'

'You're smelling better by the minute, feller.'

'I beg your pardon?'

'On account of not talking bullshit.'

Another day and a night passed after Fort Randall was astern of the *Delta Dawn*. The stern-wheeler, virtually empty of combustible cargo and almost completely stripped of everything wooden that was not essential to keep her afloat and under-way and give shelter to those aboard, had the river to herself. They were beyond Fort Thompson then, heading for Fort Pierre. There was still a lengthy and relatively well-populated stretch of river ahead, to Fort Bulford on the Dakotas-Montana line: but it was the weather and water conditions that held most other boats at their moorings.

The sky was leaden with low clouds, poised to race and unload their threat of snow when the next norther was unleashed from beyond the Canadian border. On either bank, the Missouri was already frozen solid, the new ice trapping the larger floes which had drifted down from the north. The boat was constantly breaking thin ice, which immediately re-formed again when the water astern became calm beyond the wake from the paddle-wheel.

It was mid-morning when the roustabout with the beer-gut put the *Delta Dawn* aground on a sandspit.

Edge was in the wheel-house, taking a turn at pilot. Linn and Rhett were outside on the port and starboard superstructure. The channel of thin ice at midstream was about a hundred feet wide. To either side of this was a strip of thick ice, extending the bank some thirty or so feet into the river. On each bank there was a heavy growth of mixed fir, pine and spruce with only the taller brush showing above the thick layer of snow.

The half-breed saw the hump of the sandbank, lengthways along the river, in line with the port side of the boat.

'Go left,' he instructed and the helmsman complied, turning the wheel to swing the bow towards the eastern bank.

'Straight ahead, feller.'

111

The boat veered again, with ample water between her starboard side and the ice: and enough room to stay clear of the sand.

Until her bow drew level with the nearest end.

She was still going at full speed, cracking ice with her prow and thrashing up white water astern.

The helmsman spun her wheel hard over and she hit the sand with an audible smack. Her bow reared out of the water and she came to an abrupt halt, the impact sending a violent judder down her whole length. The paddle-wheel continued to thrash at the river, broiling it to white spume but unable to make way.

'You're through, you bastards!' the helmsman bellowed.

Like everyone else aboard, he and Edge had been shoved forward by the abruptness of the halt. But the roustabout had been prepared for the impact and had the wheel for support. He also had a Colt in his coat pocket.

Edge had to regain his balance and stoop to pick up his fallen Winchester. He had turned and was pumping the lever action as the roustabout leapt backwards and levelled the cocked revolver.

'The South will –'

His knuckle whitened around the trigger. But the explosion was too loud for a revolver. And there was no smoke or muzzle flash.

At first, a hail of broken glass as the starboard windows of the wheel-house were blasted into a million splinters. Then the roustabout's head disintegrated. One instant his face glared hatred towards Edge. The next there was the bloody stump of his neck and nothing above it.

The beheaded corpse crumpled. The windows on the port side of the wheel-house suffered the same fate as the others. But, on the frames and the shards of glass that remained, there was liquid crimson: oozing and bubbling, then freezing. Dotted here and there were fragments of solid tissue.

Rhett's shocked face appeared in the shattered and blood-sprayed framework. The pallor of the rest of his complexion emphasised the red-rims and dark bags that exhaustion had given his eyes.

'Sonofabitch, what was that?' he shrieked.

Edge shifted his gaze to the other window and saw Linn scowling into the wheel-house, the sawn-off shotgun still aimed and smoking from both barrels.

Down below, the engineer disengaged the drive and the paddle-wheel ceased to beat at the water.

'Obliged to you,' Edge told the Negro. 'Makes two I owe you for.'

'Never could count worth a damn, suh,' Linn growled, breaking the gun open and flipping out the spent cartridge cases.

'You could have killed me!' Rhett accused. 'You realise that, boy?'

Linn pressed fresh cartridges into the twin breech and snapped the shotgun closed. 'About all I can do in that line is figure out Mr Edge counts more than you do, mister!' he snarled.

Charity raced up the stairway from the Hurricane Deck, followed closely by the rest of the oddly-assorted crew. 'What happened?' the woman demanded.

'I almost got killed, that's what!' Rhett snorted.

Edge stepped across the wheel-house, put the engine telegraph to STOP and moved around the headless corpse to go outside.

Charity peered in through the smashed window on the starboard side and made a retching noise when she saw the dead man. 'How disgusting!' she shrieked, whirling away from the gruesome sight and covering her mouth with her hands. 'What a horrible way to die!'

Edge shifted his expressionless eyes for a final look at the dead man: the body unmarked below chest level, but the stump of the neck and the coat at his shoulders stained bright crimson with slick, still oozing blood.

He spat into the hard-packed snow on the decking. 'Sure enough came to one sticky end, ma'am.'

A howitzer exploded the threat of further death towards the helpless *Delta Dawn*.

CHAPTER TWELVE

The shell sped through the freezing air with a high-pitched whistle. A solid shot, it cracked out of the timber on the south bank of the river, smashed down on to the solid ice, bounced high and arced over the forward Hurricane Deck canopy.

'They got artillery!' This from the silver miner with a beard. 'They got friggin' artillery.'

'Twelve pounder, I figure,' his normally smooth-shaven but now heavily bristled companion growled.

From deep in the timber came the strident blast of a bugle sounding the charge. Then a fusillade of rifle shots and a chorus of screaming battle-cries.

'They got a whole friggin' army!' the young steward shrieked as everyone else near the wheel-house and on the stairway started to move.

Many of the wildly fired bullets thudded into the trunks of intervening trees. Some ricochetted and a few reached the river clear of obstruction. And the *Delta Dawn* suffered her first battle scars at the hands of the enemy.

The blond-haired youngster seemed petrified by fear. His mouth stayed open after the shouted words and he remained half-turned from the waist: staring with wide eyes into the timber. He flinched with the spasms of fear as each bullet thudded into the hull and superstructure of the stern-wheeler.

As the half-breed sprinted past the boy, he curled out his free hand, hooked it around the waist and lifted him clear of the decking.

'Catch!' he yelled.

Another volley of shots exploded through the timber, to the accompaniment of a new burst on the bugle: this time off-key.

Ferris and Charity, Rhett and the miners and the European roustabout were already across the Hurricane Deck and starting down the next stairway. Linn and the young crewman with the old eyes were trailing.

114

They crouched and Edge ducked under the new hail of lead. .

Both stacks were holed, woodwork was peppered and glass shattered across the lower deck from smashed windows.

The treads of the stairway were slippery with hard-packed snow. The two roustabouts below looked up and saw Edge had the now struggling steward under one arm and the Winchester fisted in his other hand.

'Now, suh!' Linn roared, running forward and releasing the shotgun, throwing out his arms to receive the youngster.

Edge swung sideways-on to the head of the stairway and used the momentum of the turn and a shove with his hip to hurl the heavier burden away from him.

The boy arced through mid-air, kicking his legs, flailing his arms and screaming. Something glinted in his right hand: even in the dull light under the low, dark clouds.

The Negro braced himself on slightly bent legs.

Edge started down the stairway. On the periphery of his vision he glimpsed a scene that triggered the loudest and clearest echo of war. But there was no time for a double take to confirm that the components were real and not figments of a snow-mirage. For, directly ahead of him, a man was aiming a Winchester – at Linn.

The half-breed snatched his free hand off the stairway rail, fisted it around the barrel of the rifle and fired from the hip.

The Negro accepted the flying weight of the steward.

Two rifles exploded together – their simultaneous cracks masked by a second firing of the howitzer.

The black man grunted, staggered backwards and fell hard to his rump. Blood stained both the front and rear of his right upper arm. But he continued to hold the screaming steward.

The cylinder and several arms of the boat's paddle-wheel were splintered by the solid shot from the artillery piece.

The bearded miner had been crouching on the top step of the lower stairway. Edge's bullet penetrated the centre of his forehead and exploded into air again amid a rain of gore at the nape of his neck. And the second Southern sympathiser who elected to stay aboard the *Delta Dawn* fell limply to the stairs and slithered down to the forward Main Deck.

Charity Meagher's scream of horror sounded above a third volley of rifle shots from the shore.

Edge reached the Hurricane Deck in a crouch. The young

roustabout with the old eyes threw himself out at full length and bellied across the deck.

'They said they'd give us a chance to get off!' the steward shrieked. 'Bastards, bastards, bastards!'

He was still writhing across the massive form of Linn. As he repeated the oath for the third time, he raised his right arm high and plunged it downwards. At the instant of the change of direction, Edge and Linn both saw the knife clutched in the youngster's fist.

The Negro snarled and flung up his good arm. Edge cursed softly and exploded a shot towards the third member of the Rebels' fifth column. A hole showed high in his back, left of centre. Dark staining blossomed.

Wind gusted the freezing air.

Flakes of snow fell.

The steward became still, but not before a dying movement of his knife hand had sunk the blade through Linn's coat sleeve and cut a furrow in the fabric and the flesh below, from wrist to elbow.

'I never thought that little punk was a traitor, suh!' Linn croaked through gritted teeth as Edge hauled the corpse off the Negro and helped the twice-injured man to his feet.

The snow fell harder, slanted close to the horizontal by the strengthening wind.

'If you'll overlook the expression,' the half-breed growled as he picked up the shotgun, 'only figured two niggers in the woodpile myself. I counted wrong, but I reckon we're even.'

Linn's right arm hung limply at his side. But he was able to take the shotgun with his left hand.

'Whatever you say, suh.'

A third solid shot from the howitzer smashed through the wheel-house.

Rifle shots, muted by the rising howl of the new norther, thudded bullets into wood and against metal from one end of the *Delta Dawn* to the other.

'I say we get the hell off this ship!' the half-breed snapped, and led the way in a low crouch across the Hurricane Deck and down the stairway.

On the forward Main Deck he turned right and lunged into the cover of the starboard boiler-room bulkhead. The body of the bearded miner was already covered with a coating of fresh snow.

The other miner was sheltering from the Rebel fire. The two

116

roustabouts, Henry Rhett, Horace Ferris and Charity Meagher were also huddled in solid cover – the men clutching Winchesters and the woman pressing both hands to her left breast, where the reason for the slaughter was sewn.

'You see them, Captain?' Rhett yelled, his voice high-pitched with excitement. 'Just like Bob wrote me it was in the war.'

Edge had seen them. At least a score of men making what speed they could through the deep snow and tangled brush of the timber. Men in the grey and yellow uniforms of the old Confederacy. One with the insignia of a Colonel who brandished his sabre as he advanced. Another clutching a bugle. A third holding aloft the Rebel flag with its emblem of a thirteen-starred cross. Dismounted cavalry advancing on foot under the covering fire of an expertly manned twelve-pounder howitzer hidden far back in the trees. No more than three hundred yards back from the target judging by the gun-crew's effectiveness in locating and hitting the helplessly stranded *Delta Dawn*.

The half-breed had seen many similar sights during the War Between the States. But with one vital difference – this new breed of Rebels were not armed with single-shot carbines. They had Winchester repeaters. Many more of them than the handful of defenders aboard the stern-wheeler.

'Vhat is wrong with Jack Linn?' the European with the battered face gasped.

'His arms!' Ferris yelled above the howl of the wind.

Edge glanced at the Negro, who had dropped the shotgun and was leaning hard against the bulkhead, both his coat sleeves stiff with frozen blood. 'Got a hole in one,' the half-breed muttered. 'The other's badly sliced.'

The howitzer fired again and the port stack toppled against its twin. The howling wind snatched at the acrid smoke and swirled it down through the stinging snow.

'Let's go!' Edge yelled as belching smoke and slanting snow reduced visibility to just a few feet.

'Where?' Charity demanded.

'Off of here. Fast.'

He dragged one of her hands away from her breast and lunged forward. The woman shrieked and was forced to go after him. All but one of the men sprinted in their wake. Out of the cover of the boiler room, across the deck and to the port bow.

117

'Jump!' he yelled over his shoulder.

Like an automaton, she leapt over the gunwale, her left hand still gripped tightly in his big fist. The blizzard tugged at them and blinded them to everything more than a yard away. Their feet hit hard on the frozen sandspit. Charity almost stumbled but kept her footing as she was forced to continue the sprint.

Rifle fire punctured the howl of the wind. Their boots cracked ice, and water rose to their ankles. Edge tripped and the woman fell alongside him – both on the strip of thick ice that extended out from the bank.

Behind them, Ferris, Rhett, the miner and two roustabouts made the safety of the ice.

'We're going towards them, Captain!' Rhett shrieked.

'Nothing's ever won running away, feller,' Edge snarled as they all got to their feet and started to run again – on a diagonal line from the reared up bow of the *Delta Dawn*. To take them out of the line of fire between the timber and the stern-wheeler.

In the deep snow covering the solid ground between the trees, Edge halted and the others imitated him: leaning against trunks and crouching to catch their breath.

'I'm impressed by your gallantry, Edge,' Charity gasped, snatching her hand away to massage it. 'But I'll be safe here. You'll be able to kill easier without me as a burden.'

The half-breed refastened his grip on her. His blue eyes, narrowed to the thinnest of slits, looked even more like chips of ice against the snowflakes clinging to his bristles. 'Ain't gallantry, lady,' he snarled. 'You got the letter.'

'Vhere is Jack Linn?'

'Sure ain't with us,' Rhett responded after a fast glance around. His laugh had a hint of hysteria in it. 'He's one guy we'd be sure to see in all this snow.'

The group had to shout at each other to be heard above the howl of the wind: far louder in the timber as the norther ripped between the trunks. The only sounds which were louder came from the muzzle of the howitzer and the barrels of the Rebel's rifles.

'Dead, I'll warrant!' Ferris snarled.

'No guarantees were issued,' Edge growled, jerking Charity away from the tree against which she was leaning.

He gave no order and this was another echo of war. Then there had been troopers – six in particular – who accepted and respected their captain's detachment from themselves in special circumstances. They followed in the knowledge that they could trust him and the awareness that he would communicate with them if it proved necessary.

. Today, amid the snow and wind of a Dakotas blizzard, a woman had no alternative but to follow him. And five men trusted him because there was nothing else they could do.

Edge moved without the sense of exhilaration that had gripped him during the heat of battles fought many years ago. His pace was as fast as possible through the snow and with the reluctant woman struggling in his grip. But his mind was working at a measured progress, receiving the information given by the regular roar of the howitzer and programming the direction he should take.

He struck due south for a long time, then swung east. The reports from the artillery piece were louder. Rifle-fire could hardly be heard at all.

He halted and all those behind him were grateful for the rest.

'See nothing happens to her, feller,' Edge said, close to the ear of Ferris, and released the woman.

Then he drew the razor, dropped the Winchester into the snow and pointed at Rhett, the roustabout with the battered face and the young one with the old eyes. He beckoned that they should follow him, and then put the stiff finger to his lips.

The four men advanced in line abreast, Rhett with the blade of his Apache Knuckleduster extended and the other two with Colts drawn.

The howitzer was positioned ten yards from where Edge had called the halt. It was an old Napoleon, a twelve-pounder mounted on a modified twenty-four-pounder carriage. The wheels of the carriage were deeply imbedded in frozen snow. There was a three-man crew – one passing the shot, another loading and a third firing. A corporal and two enlisted men.

The Rebel who was loading saw the intruders loom up through the blizzard. His youthful face was abruptly contorted by terror and his mouth gaped wide to vent a shriek of warning.

Two revolvers cracked and the face was suddenly sheened with bright crimson flooding from wounds in the cheek.

Edge lunged at the corporal and Rhett went towards the third man. Both the Rebels were caught as they spun around. Rhett's blade sank deep into the chest of the enlisted man. He withdrew it as he followed the corpse down, folded it into his

119

fist and began to punish the dead face with the brass knuckles.

The half-breed killed the non-com with a sideways slash of the razor, the blade gashing open the taut throat, the windpipe and the jugular vein. As the man crumpled, Edge still wore a grin of satisfaction. It stayed in place as he looked down at Rhett: kneeling on the chest of the corpse and sending up a spray of blood from the mutilated face with each thudding punch.

'He ain't feeling no pain, Rhett!' Edge snapped.

It brought an end to the beating. 'You would, if I could bring myself to do it, Captain!' Rhett snarled, staggering to his feet. 'You killed Bob and all his buddies. I heard the story.' He pointed his blood-caked hand down at the pulped face of the dead man. 'But I owe you too much. So I just imagined he was you!'

'Killed his buddies is all, feller,' Edge yelled above the storm as the two roustabouts stared at him. 'Would have killed him, but they did it first. Don't believe all you hear.'

'Hold your fire!' a voice yelled from beyond the curtain of slanting snow. 'Colonel says to cease fire. We're gonna board.'

A uniformed figure ran into view and came to an abrupt halt. 'Damnation!' he exclaimed.

Rhett's tiny gun exploded and the man staggered backwards, hit a tree and collapsed, a blossom of blood showing the position of his heart.

'Maybe,' Edge growled. 'But figure to keep it one nation.'

'I believe you, Captain,' Rhett said, out of context now.

There was a deafening roar: far louder than the several reports exploded by the howitzer. A ball of fire glowed through the trees and the falling snow for an instant. Then the stench of burning touched the nostrils of the men and was immediately swamped by the wetness of the blizzard.

'The boat?' the European roustabout asked. 'You think they have blown up the *Delta Dawn*?'

'Them or a feller a hell of a lot worse armed,' Edge growled.

He spun around and lunged back to where Ferris, Charity and the miner waited. Only the woman did not express relief at seeing him.

'What was that?' the miner asked.

'A report,' the half-breed tossed at him, then snatched up his Winchester and grabbed the woman's hand again. 'But I ain't reading nothing into it until I check for myself.'

He started another struggling run through the timber and

was again trailed by the men. This time it was easier, for he was able to follow the beaten tracks made by the advancing Rebels. All rifle-fire had ceased now and there was no glow from the river as they drew closer. Pieces of charred lumber and twisted metal began to mark the snow. Then torn-off portions of human flesh and entire bodies. Where the trees ended and the thick ice of the river began there was more debris of the same kind. Wedged into the leafless branches of some high brush was a head. The crinkled hair had been seared from the skull and the eyes had melted in their sockets. But the basic structure of the face remained the same as it had been in life. The skin had been black before the flames touched it.

'He blew her boilers, that is vhat happened,' the battered-face roustabout pronounced sadly as, like the others, he turned away from the severed head to peer out through the slanting snow to try to see what remained of the *Delta Dawn*. 'Jack, he must have shut down all the escape valves. No one else vould hear the noise she vas making in this storm.'

'It is the bravest of the brave who die for their country,' Ferris said pompously.

Edge eased his grip on Charity's hand. 'You gonna be that brave?' he asked evenly.

Every head was wrenched around to stare at him. The woman jerked free of the half-breed.

'What?' she shrieked.

He showed her a cold, evil grin. 'You been trying too hard not to come with me.'

'Edge!' Ferris snarled.

The half-breed started to swing his Winchester towards the terrified woman: not fast.

Charity responded with speed and strength. Her foot lashed out to kick the rifle from his loose grasp. Then she whirled and lunged away from the solid ground of the bank. Her violent action trapped the other men into immobility for a vital moment. And in that time she was on the ice and swallowed up by the blizzard.

'Women never were no good!' Henry Rhett howled, and ran forward. He pushed his feet apart and slithered across the ice. And disappeared into the falling snow faster than the woman had done.

'Charity!' Ferris shrieked, still staring at Edge.

'You notice how she almost threw up every time a Rebel got his?'

121

The woman screamed.

'I got the she-cat, Captain!'

The half-breed ignored the questions fired at him by Ferris and led the way out over the frozen river, picking a careful course across the ice and around the scattered debris of the explosion.

Rhett had knocked down Charity a few yards short of where the thick ice ended and the water was still trying to freeze around the sandspit. She was flat on her back. Rhett was erect, a foot on her belly and the muzzle of his Winchester against her throat. There was a triumphant grin on his weakly handsome face. Charity's lovely features were made ugly by a scowl of hatred.

'How did you know?' she gasped as the men gathered around her.

'You ran, lady,' Edge told her. 'Didn't know anything until then. Just suspected.'

'Why, Charity?' Ferris choked.

'To kill Coolidge, that's why!' she snarled, not struggling under the booted foot and the rifle muzzle. Insane triumph merged with the hatred in her eyes as she swept her gaze around each towering man in turn. 'The letter's a fake, you fools! With it I was able to wipe out every Government agent in New Orleans. And I almost got close enough to your stinking President to blow him off the face of the earth!'

'But the attempts on my life?' Ferris rasped desperately, and waved his arms about him. 'All this?'

'The brave, magnificent innocents!' she rasped, the look of triumph draining from her face. 'They were misled in the same way you were. But they served their purpose. Their actions ensured Coolidge would meet us. And I asked nothing of them I would not do myself. I was prepared to die in completing my mission.'

'How about before completion, lady?' Rhett growled.

'You were working for the Rebels all those months you were engaged to John?' Ferris demanded.

Tears squeezed from her eyes and froze in the snow on her cheeks. But she was not weeping for John Ferris. Perhaps for the Rebels who had died – or maybe in response to the reality of defeat.

Ferris leaned forward, as if he was about to crouch down beside her. Instead, his arm shot out and the heel of his hand chopped down against the hammer of Rhett's Winchester.

122

The gun discharged its bullet and blasted a powder-burned hole in the centre of the woman's throat. The expression of sadness remained on her face in death and her green eyes stayed open, glazed by frozen tears.

'She failed with the President,' Ferris told the startled Rhett. 'But she was responsible for the death of my son.'

'No sweat, Mr Ferris,' Rhett assured with a thin smile. 'One less female to compete with me. Mind if I take the letter for a souvenir?'

He released the Winchester and dropped into a crouch. The combination weapon came out from under his coat and he extended the blade to cut at the coat, dress and underwear of Charity Meagher.

'You will both receive the balance of the fee I offered,' Ferris said dully.

'Damn right,' Edge muttered. 'I ain't the kind that makes grand gestures.'

Ferris nodded. 'I am quite aware of that, sir. Which is why I have a greater admiration for the Negro. Even for these misguided men who died for a cause they believed in. True patriots.'

'Put that on their grave markers, feller. Sure ain't enough of them left to put names to.'

The group of standing men watched as Rhett pulled the cut clothing away from the body of the woman to expose her firm, dark-crested breasts. The stooping man bent closer to pick at the new stitching in the bodice of the dress.

And died.

The rifle shot was exploded from short range by a man attired in the uniform of a Confederate cavalry sergeant. There was blood on his face and at his belly. He was already toppling forward as he squeezed the trigger of his Winchester. His eyes displayed death before he hit the ice.

Rhett was a corpse an instant before this, the bullet of the dying man smashing through the crown of his head, penetrating his brain and lodging in his throat. The impact of the lead pushed him backwards across the ice. Blood trailed his course. His feet, legs and hips went off the ice and into the water. Thin ice cracked. His centre of gravity moved over the unfrozen river and his entire body sank into it.

'All for a lousy souvenir!' the younger crewman growled.

Edge relaxed after the tension of swinging his rifle towards Rhett's killer. His eyes shifted momentarily to the naked

123

breasts of the dead woman, already frosted with fresh snow. 'Guess that's what's called a booby trap,' he muttered, and turned for the bank.

'Where are you going?' the miner asked anxiously.

'Find out if the Rebs had horses to go with the cavalry uniforms,' the half-breed answered. 'Figure they had to have some. To haul the gun.'

'I'd like to remain here for awhile, if I may?' Ferris asked, crouching down beside Charity.

'Be a four and a half grand gesture to come back for you,' Edge told him.

The two crewmen and the miner went with the half-breed. They found the horses – saddled and with bags bulged by supplies of food – a hundred yards behind the howitzer emplacement. The others waited, hunched in their coats, while Edge led two geldings back to the river.

There was a smile of satisfaction on his lean face, visible through the snowflakes clinging to his eyebrows and bristles. He had a horse again and had survived while others died. Soon he would have enough money to secure his independence for a long time to come. The blizzard in wild, open country was easier to take than when the norther had unleashed snow on the civilisation of Omaha.

Ferris had left the body of the woman and was standing close to the bow of the *Delta Dawn*. The wind veered just once, and for part of a second the moving curtain of pelting snow parted. The stern-wheeler was seen for that moment: little more than a hull supporting tangled heaps of wreckage, a lot of it charred as black as the man who had struck the final blow at her. She was solidly wedged in surrounding ice now.

'Self-sacrifice is laudable,' Ferris said sadly as Edge led the two horses out on to the snow-covered ice. 'But it is important that men of ability stay alive to fight new battles.'

Off the port bow of the crippled boat, the body of Henry Rhett was visible: full-length and face up – as if trapped in a state of suspended animation by the clear ice against the sand-pit.

'He served in his own way, Mr Edge,' Ferris went on when the half-breed remained silent. 'He was a pervert. A lot of things a man should not be.'

'He was okay,' Edge allowed with a trace of feeling in his

124

voice. Then he showed a faint grin. 'Relative to another feller I used to know.'

'He's not the kind I'd usually sing the praises of, but – '

'If you have to,' the half-breed growled, holding the reins of both horses in one hand so that he could touch the brim of his hat in a gesture of farewell to the body caught in the ice, 'freeze a jolly good fellow.'

The George G. Gilman
Appreciation Society

is now operating from
Mr David Whitehead,
4 Key Close,
Tower Hamlets, London, E.1. 4HG

Please send an SAE for details

NEL BESTSELLERS